INGRID *and the* WOLF

INGRID *and the* WOLF

ANDRÉ ALEXIS

Tundra Books

Published in Canada by Tundra Books,
481 University Avenue, Toronto, Ontario M5G 2E9

Published in the United States by Tundra Books of Northern New York,
P.O. Box 1030, Plattsburgh, New York 12901

Library of Congress Control Number: 2004117238

Library and Archives Canada Cataloguing in Publication

Alexis, André, 1957-
    Ingrid and the wolf / Andre Alexis.

ISBN 0-88776-691-9

        I. Title.

PS8551.L474I54 2005   JC813'.54   C2004-907227-7

We acknowledge the financial support of the Government
of Canada through the Book Publishing Industry
Development Program (BPIDP) and that of the
Government of Ontario through the Ontario Media
Development Corporation's Ontario Book Initiative. We
further acknowledge the support of the Canada Council
for the Arts and the Ontario Arts Council for our publishing program.

ONTARIO ARTS COUNCIL
CONSEIL DES ARTS DE L'ONTARIO

Design: Terri Nimmo

Printed in Canada

3 4 5 6   10 09 08 07 06

To: Nicola
         Talia
         Naomi
         Hannah

         With Love

INGRID *and the* WOLF

1

Ingrid Balazs

There was once a girl named Ingrid Balazs.

Ingrid lived with her parents, Sandor and Krysztina, in a neighborhood called Parkdale. They lived in a small flat in a house on Cowan and, because they were poor, they were very frugal.

Sandor Balazs worked in Rosedale, a wealthy neighborhood. He worked as a gardener in the home of August Dawes, an architect who was unpredictable and a little thoughtless. Mr. Dawes once fired four butlers in a day: the first because the man lisped, the second because his shoes were scuffed, the third because he'd called him

Auggy, and the fourth because August Dawes found it distracting to speak to a man with bad teeth.

Still . . . Sandor and Mr. Dawes got on very well. Each seemed to understand the other and, just as important, each was comfortable in the other's presence.

Krysztina Balazs worked for a kind but stingy woman named Ashley Montague. Ms. Montague was a tax lawyer, and Krysztina kept her home clean, washed her clothes, and prepared her meals. In the years Krysztina had worked for Ms. Montague, they'd spoken to each other not more than a handful of times, but once a year, without fail, Ms. Montague raised Krysztina's salary by four cents an hour.

As both of her parents worked, Ingrid spent a lot of time alone. From three thirty till seven, on weekdays, Ingrid was home by herself.

It was a fine arrangement.

Or, rather, it was fine for Ingrid's parents. For Ingrid, it was more complicated. She enjoyed being on her own, free to eat a little of whatever was in the fridge. But then, she was not often hungry and, besides, once she finished her homework, she felt lonely. They had no television, no CD player, and Ingrid had very few toys.

"You should read more," her father would say. "It will improve your mind and make you self-reliant." But there was only so much reading you could do without getting bored. And only so many times you could read the novels her parents gave her – novels by Charles Dickens, mostly, and Honoré de Balzac.

On top of that, Ingrid was one of the few children at Queen Elizabeth Public who were not allowed to visit with friends after school, not so much because her parents didn't wish it but because Parkdale was a neighborhood that made her father nervous. He preferred she go straight home and stay there. Being a considerate child, that is what Ingrid did. But Ingrid couldn't help feeling her father was hiding something, that he didn't want her to play with the other children. It was as if he didn't quite approve of the neighborhood, or the school, or even Ingrid's friends. It was as if they made him uncomfortable, and Ingrid sometimes thought her father did not care about her loneliness. He was, otherwise, such a loving man, however, that she rarely thought such things for long.

2

Ingrid at School

Ingrid would not have felt quite so lonely, if things had been going well at school.

Her friendship with Alice Yee, for instance. Ingrid and Alice had known each other since kindergarten, and they'd been best friends since grade four. Now, in grade six, they were as close as sisters. And yet . . .

Alice was now friendly with Sheila Wilson.

And, as far as Ingrid could tell, Sheila Wilson wanted to own Queen Elizabeth Public School. On Sheila's first day at Queen Elizabeth, Ingrid and Alice had tried to introduce themselves. But, before they could speak,

4

Sheila said, "I'm from Prince Edward Island. It's so much nicer there, don't you think?"

And then she said, "My name's Sheila. What's yours?"

"Ingrid."

"Alice."

"I think we're going to be very good friends," said Sheila. "What have you got for lunch, Ingrid?"

"A peanut butter sandwich."

"Really?" said Sheila. "I don't like peanut butter. I think you should bring something else tomorrow."

"Why?" asked Ingrid.

"So you can share with your friends, silly. Don't you think she should share with us, Alice?"

She put one arm around Ingrid's shoulder, the other around Alice's, and together they walked into the classroom.

That first day, Sheila was almost friendly. She talked about her adorable parents, her adorable house, and her adorable Pomeranian, Spotty.

The following day, Ingrid's mother made salami sand-wiches for lunch, but Ingrid asked for peanut butter.

"You had peanut butter yesterday," said Krysztina.

"But that's what I really want," answered Ingrid.

"Oh, you girls and your whims," said Krysztina. But she made a peanut butter sandwich just for Ingrid.

In the school yard, the first person to speak to Ingrid was Sheila, Sheila followed by the two or three girls who were (already!) her entourage.

"Look," she said, "here's Ingrid. I wonder what Ingrid has for lunch. I've got egg salad. Really, I don't know why my mother bothers. I won't eat it. Here, let's see what you've got, Ingrid."

"It's peanut butter," said Ingrid.

"Didn't you tell your mother to give you something else?" asked Sheila.

"No," said Ingrid. "I asked for peanut butter."

"Why?"

"Because I love peanut butter."

"But I don't," said Sheila. "I don't have friends who eat peanut butter. If you want to be our friend, Ingrid, you'll have to do better."

"Then ... I don't know if I want to be your friend," said Ingrid.

"You hear that?" said Sheila. "She doesn't want to be our friend."

Without warning, Sheila grabbed the paper bag from Ingrid, threw the peanut butter sandwich on the ground, and danced all over it. "In Prince Edward Island, that's what we do to people who aren't friendly," said Sheila.

She stood before Ingrid, a triumphant look on her face, as if to say, *That settles things with you.*

Sheila's friends stood behind her, looking expectant, as if to ask, *Well, what are you going to do, Ingrid?*

Ingrid could barely hide her indignation. "If you ever do that again," she said finally, "you'll be very sorry."

"Ha!" said Sheila.

"Ha!" meaning, *You're just the little pigeon I thought you were, aren't you?*

For no reason, Sheila Wilson chose Ingrid to torment and, in the months that followed, she committed a handful of little cruelties. She stole Ingrid's pencils, though Ingrid had no money to replace them; threw an eraser at her back; even spat on her shoes.

It was bewildering and frustrating, but what was worse was that Alice, to whom Sheila was always kind, was friendly with Sheila and went to Sheila's house after school.

In fact, Alice thought Sheila's little tricks amusing and said, "It's just a joke, Ingrid. Sheila's not so bad, you know."

That was the worst of it – Alice did not understand, and Ingrid could not convince her Sheila was unpleasant. Ingrid felt even more alone.

Almost as bad was that, for ten months, the only thing she ate for lunch was peanut butter sandwiches. Ingrid insisted on having them, every day. It would have felt like surrender to bring anything else.

3

A Countess

And so . . .

Ingrid was lonely and she was afraid to lose her best friend. Though she knew it was important to bear troubles with dignity, it was difficult to hide her hurt and keep her temper, hard to find a good distraction.

Then, one day in January, the Balazses received a letter from the Old Country. It was in French and it said:

Dearest Sandor,
I have decided to forgive you.

It was signed: *Countess Liliane Montesquieu von Puffdorf di Turbino de la Louve des Balazs.*

The next day, they received another letter from the countess. This one, written in German, said:

> *Sandor,*
> *I have changed my mind. I do not forgive you, but I do forgive your daughter. Please send Ingrid to me, this summer, so that we may become acquainted.*

The day after that, they received yet another letter, this one in Hungarian. It said:

> *Dear Sandor,*
> *I do not know if I forgive you or not, but I might feel inclined to forgive you if I met my granddaughter.*
> *If she does not come to me this summer, I will not forgive you at all.*

Included in this letter was an airline ticket to Budapest, in Ingrid's name. She was to travel on June 28th. She was to bring nothing, save a toothbrush if she was the kind of child who brushed her teeth, and her passport. There was no return ticket.

Naturally, Ingrid was surprised.

"Who is the countess?" she asked. "And why does she have to forgive you?"

Her father answered, "She is my mother, and she is angry I married *your* mother."

Ingrid turned to her mother. "Doesn't she like you?"

"I don't think we should talk about it," her mother answered.

Ingrid turned to her father. "But, if your mother is a countess, does that mean you're a count?"

"Yes," her father answered.

"You're *Count* Balazs?"

Her father looked at her kindly, then invited her to sit on his knee. "I should have told you this sooner," he said gently. "My name is Count Sandor Ignatz Philidor Montesquieu von Puffdorf di Turbino de la Louve des Balazs. Now, finish your breakfast and get ready for school."

To his wife, Sandor said: "So, we'll tear up the ticket?"

Krysztina said: "Yes, I think we should."

"But I'd like to meet my grandmother," said Ingrid.

Sandor kissed the top of her head. "It isn't a good idea," he said. "We have chosen a different life."

"What life?"

"This life," he said.

And that seemed to be that.

Ingrid would not meet her grandmother, though Liliane Montesquieu von Puffdorf di Turbino de la Louve des Balazs was a countess and lived in the world her parents had come from.

So, she tried to put the matter out of her mind. Of course, it's very difficult to stop thinking about something once you've already thought about it.

No matter how she tried, Ingrid found herself wondering about her grandmother. What did she look like? Did a countess walk differently than other people? Did her grandmother live in a castle? Did her grandmother wear long green dresses? Did she have diamond brooches and emerald earrings?

It was so difficult to stop herself thinking these things that Ingrid spent most of the day telling herself *not* to think about castles, rubies, diamonds, servants, and all the belongings her grandmother would surely have, if she was a real countess.

And then, a few nights later, on her parents' anniversary, after her first taste of cherry kirsch, Ingrid had a most extraordinary dream.

It was so extraordinary, it needs its own chapter.

So . . .

4

Ingrid's Dream

In Ingrid's dream, she was in a house that looked very like their house on Cowan. Her parents' bedroom was where it should be. Her bedroom was as she always kept it, but it was night and she heard voices outside her door. She clearly heard someone say, "Gabor has eaten Her Highness' shoes," and then she heard the sound of a puppy mewling.

Ingrid got out of bed. The door to her room opened on its own, and out she went. There was a wolf in the hallway. It was full grown, with blue eyes and blue fur, and it stood up on its hind legs.

"Your Highness?" said the wolf.

And Ingrid, who, for some reason, did not think it strange to be called Highness, said, "Yes?"

"Did I disturb you?"

"No," said Ingrid. "I was just getting up."

"Ah," said the wolf. "I am afraid my son has eaten your slippers. He has been punished, but I fear his punishment is not enough. I offer myself in his place. Please, do with me as you see fit."

There was something frightening about the wolf. He kept a paw over his snout as he spoke, and he watched her closely. When he finished speaking, he lowered his paw and Ingrid could see his fangs, which were as long and sharp as the scissors her mother used to cut thread. The wolf sank to all fours, lowered his head, stuck out his neck, and moved closer.

Ingrid tried to step back, but the door to her room had closed and would not open. In one hand, she held a small fork; in the other, a slice of black bread. She knew she was supposed to do something, but she couldn't remember what. Being kind, she offered the bread to the wolf.

This was not the thing to do.

The wolf rose from the carpet and let out a most frightening howl. "What is your name?" he snarled.

But Ingrid was so frightened she couldn't speak, and she couldn't remember her name.

"Allison?" she whispered.

"What?" the wolf cried.

"Giselle?" she whispered.

The wolf rose up on his hind legs, and he was taller than he had been. The back of his neck touched the ceiling.

"Wanda?" Ingrid whispered. "Samantha? Judith? Melissa?"

As she spoke, Ingrid turned away from the wolf and tried desperately to open the door to her bedroom. She pulled at the doorknob. She pushed, but the door wouldn't budge.

She felt the wolf's breath on her neck and then, mercifully, she woke up.

5

Sunday Nights

Ingrid didn't dream about the wolf *every* night.

For months she had the same dream, but only on *Sunday* nights. Always the same: the wolf, the slender fork, the black bread. And she always woke at the same point, just as the wolf breathed on her neck.

It was so frightening, she did not like to sleep on Sundays. She would lie in her narrow bed, say her prayers, and think of things that keep you awake: birthday presents, new dresses, things funny, things sad. . . . Nothing worked. She would fall asleep and she would be back in the same place, with the same wolf, the same fork, the same black bread.

Naturally, her parents noticed how tired she was on Monday mornings, but they did nothing until, one Monday morning, her father asked if she was all right.

"Is everything okay, sweetheart?"

"Yes," said Ingrid.

"Is everything okay at school?"

"Yes," she said (quickly).

"There isn't something you want to tell me?"

Ingrid didn't want to upset her parents, but she said, "Well . . . there is something. . . ."

"What is it, darling?"

"I'm having . . . I'm having nightmares."

Krysztina, who was sewing at the breakfast table, pricked her thumb with the needle. She looked up at her daughter. "Is it the wolf?" she asked.

Ingrid was astonished.

"Yes," she said. "How did you know?"

Both Sandor and Krysztina stopped what they were doing and stared at her. Sandor was first to speak. "Did you give him the fork?" he asked.

"No," said Ingrid. "I always give him the bread."

Her father looked at her in horror.

"But you mustn't," said Sandor.

"Why not?"

"It is a great insult," her father answered.

A drop of blood ran from the tip of Krysztina's thumb to her wrist. "It's eight thirty," she said. "We'll talk about this tonight."

Ingrid went to her room to put on her winter dress, which she hated because it was even smaller than her summer dress and pinched wherever it touched her. But, despite the dress, she felt relief. It was comforting that her parents knew of the dream. It was as if she'd told a terrifying secret and then found it wasn't so terrifying after all.

That night, when they all sat down for supper, Sandor said, "I had the same dream, when I was your age. And my mother had it, and her father, and . . . every Balazs has had it."

"Not every Balazs," said Krysztina.

"No, that's true. Not *every* Balazs."

"But what does it mean?" asked Ingrid.

"It means you are my daughter," said Sandor. "And your home is calling you."

"But *this* is my home," said Ingrid.

"It is one of your homes," said Krysztina. "The other one is calling."

Ingrid was confused. How could you be called by a place you didn't know?

"It's nothing to be afraid of," said Sandor. "We live here, far away from wolves and that world."

But what was the Old World like? Ingrid wondered.

"Your dream will pass," said Sandor.

And Krysztina said, "Until it does, you can sleep with us."

Which is just what Ingrid did.

Every Sunday night, she would sleep on the bed between her mother and father, which was good for her, but not so good for her parents. Ingrid was a restless sleeper who would, inevitably, turn around in the bed so that, by night's end, her feet were in her parents' faces (eyes, noses, mouths) and her head was at their knees.

The nightmares did not stop, but it was comforting to wake in her parents' arms.

6

The Old World

In the months that followed Liliane's letter, Ingrid found it difficult to think of anything but the Old Country.

What did it look like?

Was it filled with servants, stone walls, and strange trees? The most peculiar tree Ingrid knew was the willow, so she imagined her grandmother, Countess Liliane, in an arbor filled with willows, being served lunch . . . and what was lunch in the Old Country? Cucumber sandwiches with parsley, lemonade with honey and brown sugar, and tomato soup . . . no, not tomato soup, gazpacho . . . how wonderful it would be to sit in an arbor and eat gazpacho.

Ingrid could not imagine preferring anywhere to Toronto, but . . . still . . . she was not altogether happy in Toronto just now. She'd learned that Alice and her family were leaving for the summer, going to Hawaii. That meant, for the summer, there would be no sleepovers at the Yees', no camping trips with the Yees, nothing to relieve the solitude. In fact, it consoled Ingrid to think there was a place where her family (and she herself, perhaps) was well regarded, a place where they (and she herself, certainly) were countesses and counts, and a place she could go to, if only . . .

The more Ingrid thought about this, the more she wondered if her parents weren't mistaken. Surely it was right for her to visit Countess Liliane? Right or not, Ingrid filled pages in her schoolbooks, pages in her diary, any blank pages she could find, with fanciful and detailed drawings of manors and chateaux where, she imagined, a countess might live.

One evening, Ingrid said, "Dad? What's your mother like?"

"She is very stubborn," said Sandor.

"Do you miss her?"

"I do, yes, but what can we do? She refuses to visit us."

"Do you love her?"

"Of course," he answered.

For a moment, though, he seemed sad, as if it hurt to recall his mother, his childhood, the country where he was born.

"Does she love you?" asked Ingrid.

"I believe she does," said Sandor. "But we have had a disagreement. We haven't seen each other for some time."

How strange, thought Ingrid, that parents and children should not speak. She could not imagine a time when she would not wish to speak to her parents.

"But she wants me to visit her?" asked Ingrid.

"So it seems," said Sandor. "My mother is not ready to see me as yet."

But, thought Ingrid, what if I can convince her to see her son?

As it was, summers were long and dull, even with the Yees in town. The very idea of summer made her uncomfortable. *Yes.* The more Ingrid thought about it, the more it seemed the thing to do: She must visit her grandmother, even though her parents were set against it.

Ingrid searched for the letters her grandmother had sent. She wasn't certain why she wanted to see them. She could read neither French nor German, though she spoke a little of each. Perhaps it was only to reassure herself there truly was a Countess Liliane Montesquieu von Puffdorf di Turbino de la Louve des Balazs.

Her father couldn't recall where he'd put the letters. "In the chest of drawers?"

This was typical of her father. He was careless with bills, letters, reminders, and notices to be signed. He assumed they would be seen to by others more capable than he was. His wife, for instance.

But it was while searching for Liliane's letters that Ingrid discovered her father hadn't thrown her plane ticket out, after all. He had ripped it in two and left it in a paper bag in the bathroom. The bag had fallen behind the laundry basket and it was here Ingrid discovered it.

"Did you find your grandmother's letters?" asked Sandor.

"No," said Ingrid.

Sandor smiled. "Perhaps it's just as well," he said. "You are certain to get others from your grandmother. My mother dislikes the telephone. It's too modern. When she wishes, she'll send you more letters."

Ingrid did not tell him she'd found her ticket. She kept it secret.

She taped the two pieces of the ticket together and hid it in her math book . . . near the back page, beside the multiplication tables — her favorite page because she loved the number nine: 9, 18, 27, 36, one side rising as the other falls.

She was to leave Toronto on the 28th of June, and this was reassuring but, from the moment she hid the ticket, Ingrid was anxious.

First, there was the dream she had on Sundays, a frightening distraction.

Then, there were her parents. Though she thought it was right to leave, she couldn't see *how* to go without their permission and she felt wicked keeping the ticket from them.

So, it was a relief when June finally came and she herself received a letter from Countess Liliane. The letter was addressed to *Countess Ingrid Balazs*. It was in English and it said:

My dear Ingrid,
I look forward to meeting you.

On Sunday, June 29th, my servant, Laszlo, will meet you in Budapest, and he will accompany you to your, perhaps, rightful home. Laszlo will see to anything you need.

Please feel free to strike him, should you wish conversation. He will bring along a stick for that purpose. (Though I am certain I need not tell you, please do not strike Laszlo anywhere but on his back, unless you must.)

Yours,
Countess Liliane

When Ingrid read the letter to her parents, her father was moved. "How wonderful," he said. "Laszlo is still alive."

"But why would I hit him?" asked Ingrid.

Her father smiled fondly. "Laszlo can't speak unless you hit him," he said. "He has a medical condition. He must be struck on the back every few hours, so he can speak. I am sorry you will not meet him this summer."

Ingrid did not know what to say.

But what did it matter? Though she didn't know *how* she would go, Ingrid was convinced she would be going to Budapest and Liliana, so convinced that she told Alice.

"What's in Liliana?" asked Alice.

"I don't know," said Ingrid, "but I'll try to bring something back."

7

An Imaginary Mansion

As the 28th of June approached, and with it the end of school and the start of the long summer, Ingrid grew a little desperate. She began to wonder if she should go on her own, without permission. She knew where her passport was kept. But then, how would she find Laszlo? Or how would she find her way to Liliana, if Laszlo wasn't there? No, really, without her parents' permission, it was hopeless.

She tried talking about Liliana as often as she could. "Why can't I go?" she'd ask, or, "Aren't I old enough to go by myself?"

Aside from simply asking to go, Ingrid implored, complained, suggested. She told her parents why it was important – to meet her grandmother, to bring the family back together, to have something to do for the summer, to have something interesting to tell Alice in the fall. But nothing convinced them. As soon as she spoke of Liliana or summer, her parents would smile sadly and change the subject, or they would let her speak until she had nothing more to say.

Maybe they'll change their minds by the 9th, she thought.

But the 9th of June passed and neither of her parents said anything about Liliana.

They'll change their minds by the 12th, she thought.

But the 12th passed as uneventfully as the 9th. And so passed the 13th, the 14th, and the 15th. Each day closer to the 28th was like a small sad disappointment. Until finally, on the 25th of June, having all but given up hope, Ingrid was sitting in the living room beside her father. Though there was little chance the question would lead to discussion about summer or Liliana, she asked, "Father, what was it like when you were eleven?"

Sandor answered, "It's no use talking about it, Ingrid. Your mother feels it is too dangerous for you to go to Liliana this summer."

"Why is it dangerous?"

Her father thought carefully before he answered. Then, he said, "I don't suppose it matters if I tell you. It is too late for you to go to Liliana. But you are my daughter, a Balazs. And when a Balazs reaches the age of eleven, he or she begins to dream about wolves. And when they dream about wolves, it is time for them to . . . *do* certain things."

"Did you do them?"

"Yes," said Sandor, "I did. When I was just your age. It is a tradition that goes back centuries, you see."

"Did mother . . .?"

"That is all I will say, Ingrid."

"Aren't I a real Balazs?" asked Ingrid.

She'd meant to ask: If I'm a Balazs, shouldn't I be allowed to do the things you did? But this question – Aren't I a real Balazs? – had a peculiar effect on her father. He scratched his ear. He rubbed his chin. "Perhaps you *should* go," he said slowly.

"Then I want to go," said Ingrid. "Please can I go, Father?"

"No," said Sandor. "I'm afraid we haven't got a ticket."

"But if I had a ticket, could I go?"

"Yes," said Sandor, "but you do not, and we cannot afford to buy you another."

Ingrid was not happy to tell her father about the ticket, but there were only two days before her plane left and, though she felt embarrassed at having kept a secret from her parents, she brought her father to her room, and took the ticket from the back pages of her math book.

"Here it is," she said.

Her father was stunned, but not, as you might think, by the unexpected reappearance of the ticket to Budapest, which he barely glanced at before taking it from her. What caught, and held, his attention was a drawing Ingrid had left on the bedside table. It was one of the many Ingrid had made of her imagined manors.

"Where did you get this?" asked Sandor.

It was one of the drawings Ingrid particularly liked – that of a large mansion on a hill. In front of the mansion was a well and beside the well was a tree in whose lower branches were white flowers.

"I drew it myself," she answered.

"May I have it?" asked Sandor.

And only then, after she'd given the drawing to him, did he remember her ticket. "I'm afraid I will have to take this from you," he said. "I'm sorry, but it was wrong of you to keep this a secret."

He was not angry, though. He looked at her with affection as he left her room, but that seemed to be the end of that. Now Ingrid did not even have a ticket. There was nothing to do, except face the long summer on her own.

The 26th, the last day of school, passed, and so did the 27th. Ingrid still hoped her father would say, "I've changed my mind. You should go to Liliana, if you really want to." But Sandor said no such thing. In fact, it was as if he'd forgotten all about the ticket and Liliana. He was kind to her, when he came home from work, but Ingrid was too unhappy to talk to him, to mention Liliana, or Laszlo, or anything to do with going away.

Then, at breakfast on the morning of the 28th, her mother asked, "Ingrid, this drawing is yours?"

Krysztina put Ingrid's drawing on the table before her.

"Yes," said Ingrid.

"Do you know what it is?" asked Sandor.

"It's a picture of the kind of house a countess lives in."

"Yes," said Sandor, "but it's a picture of the house I grew up in. It is the house your grandmother lives in. Where did you see it?"

"I didn't see it anywhere," said Ingrid. "I imagined it."

"What you imagined is real," said Sandor.

"You are certainly a Balazs," said Krysztina.

"If you'd like to go to Liliana, you may," said Sandor.

"It would be wrong of us to make the decision for you. Do you still want to go?"

"Yes," said Ingrid. "I *do* want to go."

"I thought so," said Sandor. "I have sent a telegram to my mother, and she has answered. Laszlo will be in Budapest when you arrive. I have borrowed Mr. Dawes' car for the day. We will take you to the airport this afternoon. Your plane leaves at six. You're certain you want to go?"

This was all very sudden and very strange for Ingrid. Before she had time to understand what was happening, it was noon, she had packed her toothbrush in a plastic box, and the three of them left for the airport. Her father drove, in Mr. Dawes' car, and she saw parts of the city she had never seen. (Well . . . she saw them, yes, but they left little impression because her excitement was such that it made time speed up.)

Ingrid and her parents spent four hours together, walking about the airport, looking at planes take off. Krysztina, in particular, was upset. She could scarcely stand to let Ingrid go and held her hand right up until it was time for Ingrid to board.

"Everything will be all right," Krysztina said. But she was saying it as much for herself as for Ingrid and, to be honest, her concern worried Ingrid more than the idea of traveling alone.

Her father accompanied her to the gate. They stood together for a few moments and then he said, "Laszlo will take you to your grandmother. You needn't worry about that. The reason my mother has asked to see you is that she wishes to know if you are a true Balazs. You will have to pass three tests, one of which is rather frightening."

"What are the tests?" said Ingrid.

"It would be unlucky for me to tell you. You must do them yourself. But you are a Balazs. You will have no trouble. Just remember, everything you do has been done by others, by me, by your grandmother. You mustn't be frightened. Remember, we love you very much."

And then, after a long hug, her father left her in the care of a stewardess, who saw to it Ingrid was at ease in the lounge before boarding.

What a peculiar feeling it was. She had given up on the summer, but here she was waiting to board a plane to Budapest. She was about to leave behind all she knew – parents, home, friends (and enemy), school. But she was not upset. She felt a lightness and excitement and, when she finally boarded the plane, she could think of nothing but how thrilling it was to go on an adventure.

The flight itself was wonderful. Her stomach fluttered as the plane rose from the ground, and then the world was beneath her, the lights of her own city touching those of the next city and the next and the next and the next. . . .

And, by the time they reached the wide black ocean, Ingrid was asleep.

8

Budapest Briefly

The stewardess woke Ingrid for breakfast.

It was day outside, but it was night for those on the plane and Ingrid was not hungry. She barely touched her warm rubbery pancakes.

The plane landed. And before she knew it, she was in the airport meeting Laszlo, an old man in a dark suit . . . with rather a lot of hair sprouting from his ears.

Then they left the airport, climbed into a black car, and passed through an old city, with its palaces, rivers, and bridges. Laszlo, at the wheel of the limousine, pointed to buildings and waterways, without slowing.

Isn't it interesting, thought Ingrid, how different

people are. What she meant was that Laszlo was not at all as she imagined him to be. He was gray-haired, thin as a reed, and friendly, though he did not say a word.

When they had been driving for some time, and there were fewer and fewer buildings by the side of the road, Ingrid, who wanted company, asked, "Did we leave Budapest?"

Laszlo stopped the limousine. He got out, opened the door on Ingrid's side, presented her with a long stick, and then bowed as deeply as his old body would allow. Ingrid was reluctant to hit him, but she hit him (gingerly) on the back, and though Laszlo looked pained, he said, "I'm so sorry, Countess. I am afraid I have a birth defect. I suffer from laringio-dorsitis. I'm afraid, Countess, that . . . how shall I say it? . . . my throat and my back are confused, you see? I cannot speak until I am struck on the back. It is very painful, and I prefer to keep silent, but if I am to speak, I must be struck every two hours. I suspect the countess will be curious about her native land, so it will not do to keep silent. I am so sorry to cause you such annoyance."

Laszlo bowed deeply, grimacing as he bowed, but he put on a brave, smiling face when he spoke to Ingrid.

"Yes," he continued. "We have left Budapest. It will be four hours before we come to the village of Lukacs."

"Are we going to Lukacs?" Ingrid asked.

Laszlo laughed politely. "Oh, no, Countess," he said. "There is nothing in Lukacs but a bear and his trainer." Then, suddenly serious, Laszlo said, "But . . . does the young countess wish to see the bear?"

"Yes," said Ingrid, "could we?"

Though she was disoriented and tired, Ingrid was curious about the country. How familiar it looked. How like a stretch of land in Southern Ontario.

Were there bears here, too?

She wanted to know everything at once, and she felt a twinge of elation as she and Laszlo drove on.

9

Puffdorf

It was a long drive to Lukacs.

Ingrid was tired, but she could not sleep.

After a while, Laszlo pointed to what looked like a small village of rickety houses, thin cows, dilapidated barns, and wild dogs. He said, "There is Puffdorf, Countess."

He said it as if she should know it.

"What's Puffdorf?" Ingrid asked.

Laszlo stopped the limousine and turned to her, to see if she were pulling his leg. He said, "The countess does not know Puffdorf?"

"No," said Ingrid.

"Ah . . . ," said Laszlo.

And he was silent.

"Wait," said Ingrid. "It's part of my name – Ingrid Montesquieu von Puffdorf di Turbino de la Louve des Balazs."

"Yes," said Laszlo. "This is where the wolves ate all the people in the village. Your father, the count, must have told you this story many times."

"Not really," said Ingrid.

In fact, her father had *never* told her of wolves eating people.

"Please tell me, Laszlo."

"As you wish," said Laszlo. "Does the countess see the burnt castle? It was during the eighteenth century, when everyone wore wigs except the peasants. It was during the eighteenth century, when no one bathed except the peasants. Noblemen covered themselves in white powder and *Kölnisch Wasser,* so no one could really smell anyone else's odd odors."

"Yes, yes," said Ingrid. "What happened with the wolves?"

"Well . . . there was a famine. The crops failed, and the cows were so thin you could lay your head in the hollow between their ribs. The peasants were dying out, and those who didn't die of hunger were eaten by the wolves, which were just as hungry as the peasants.

"The wolves were pitiless. Why, the whole town of Denes was wiped out in a single night when it was overrun by a pack of two or three hundred wolves: more wolves than there had been men, women, and children in the town."

"The wolves ate them?" asked Ingrid.

"Oh, yes," said Laszlo. "The only things people ever found in Denes were bones and hair.

"And then a child named Nadja Balazs saved Puffdorf."

"How did she save Puffdorf?" asked Ingrid.

"Well . . . Nadja's parents were poor. They couldn't afford to send their daughter away, so they kept Nadja with them wherever they went, to protect her, though they were so hungry and tired they could scarcely protect themselves.

"Now, one Sunday, while the Balazses were on the way home from church, they were surrounded by a pack of wolves. One of the wolves had already bitten her father's ankle when young Nadja took up a stick and struck the wolf.

"You wouldn't think that the best way to stop a pack of wolves, but you'd be wrong. The wolves had been having their own way for so long, it amazed them to see a girl strike one of their own. More than that, after she'd hit a few of them with her stick, young Nadja began talking to them. The wolves listened and they bowed down."

"Why did they bow down?"

"The young countess must forgive me, but I have never understood wolves. Perhaps they were astonished to find a youth who would teach them manners.

"After that, though many wolves came to Puffdorf, they never so much as touched a man, woman, or child. They ate quite a number of people in the next village, but Puffdorf was safe and sound.

"The people of Jano, the next village, did not think much of Nadja or her family. The people of Puffdorf, however, rewarded Nadja Balazs and her parents. They gave them the abandoned castle, Castle Puffdorf, and that is how the countess' family came to be called von Puffdorf."

"Am I related to Nadja?" asked Ingrid.

"Oh, yes," said Laszlo. "She is your great great great . . . great great great great . . . great great great . . . great-grandmother. The first Countess Balazs."

"How did she speak to the wolves?" Ingrid asked.

"This I do not know," answered Laszlo. "It is said the countess growled, but no one knows for certain."

"And what happened to Nadja after that?"

"She lived and then she died, Countess. But it isn't my place to say anything more. The Countess Liliane will certainly tell you all these things herself."

10

Lukacs

By the time they stopped to see the bear, Ingrid was hungry as well as tired.

She was also puzzled by Laszlo's story. It made her wonder what kind of people the Balazses actually were.

"Is the countess, my grandmother, a kind woman?" she asked.

"Oh, no," said Laszlo. "She is not kind at all. It would not be right if she were. We would all be most confused. The countess, your grandmother, is noble, which is much better. Why, just last week, two serving girls were arguing about whose day off it was — was it Marta's or was it Marfa's? – and when the countess, your grand-mother, heard them, she fired them both. You see?"

Ingrid was not sure how noble her grandmother was, but the Countess Liliane was not at all kind, clearly.

The town of Lukacs was smaller than Puffdorf, and there were more wild dogs.

When they got out of the car, the dogs seemed most interested in Ingrid. They approached to sniff at her, but Laszlo took pieces of dried meat from a leather pouch and threw them at the pack whenever the dogs got too close.

Ingrid felt a little . . . unnerved. The dogs reminded her of wolves.

There were only a dozen houses in Lukacs: a dozen houses, a gas station, a large open pit, and a bear cage that was tall and wide, with thick round black bars to keep the bear confined.

From a distance the bear looked impressive. That is, it seemed impressive to Ingrid: black, hairy, distinctly bearish. She saw its back first, as it was sitting on a little wooden stool in one corner of its cage.

As they drew closer, however, the bear began to look a little . . . mangy. Yes, it looked distinctly mangy. There were patches at the back of its head where its hair had fallen out, and it appeared to be shivering as it slept.

At least, Ingrid thought it was sleeping, but then it heard them coming and jumped up and let out a rather dismal roar. Not much of a roar at all, actually, but something closer to the *aaarrgh* a pirate might make.

"*Aaarrgh*," said the bear, and Laszlo drew back as if afraid the bear might break its cage and eat them.

Ingrid was not afraid, and she did not draw back.

She went closer, but as she did, the bear drew back from her and covered its head with a paw.

"*Aaarrgh*," it said, looking at her from beneath its paw.

Now, there was something odd about this bear. For one thing, it seemed to have blue eyes and blond eyebrows. Though Ingrid had seen very few bears, she did not think they had blond eyebrows.

Before she could investigate further, though, Laszlo took a handful of change from his pocket, threw it at the bear, and politely pulled Ingrid away from the cage.

"He hasn't been fed," said Laszlo. "It is too dangerous here."

"That isn't a bear," said Ingrid. "It's a man in a bear suit."

"Oh, the young countess is surely mistaken," said Laszlo. "This is one of the most fearsome bears I have seen in all my seventy years."

"*Aaarrgh*," said the bear.

Laszlo led Ingrid back to the car, scattering the dried meat to keep the dogs at bay.

Ingrid thought the dogs more fearsome than the bear.

As they drove away from Lukacs, she could see that Laszlo was uneasy. She said, "That wasn't a bear, was it, Laszlo?"

Laszlo sighed, and then answered, "Oh, yes, it most certainly was a bear, in my opinion. But if, for some reason, the young countess is right and it wasn't a bear, it could only be because the real bear died five years ago, and there is no other way for the people of Lukacs to make an honest living. Without a bear, they would starve and Lukacs would turn to dust. But I, Laszlo, truly believe the young countess is mistaken. The creature's roar was most frightening."

11

Countess Liliane Montesquieu von Puffdorf di Turbino de la Louve des Balazs

The countryside was most beautiful, with its hills, tree-lined lanes, houses, and cows . . . hills, lanes, cows . . . hills, lanes, cows. . . .

Ingrid was hypnotized by the land.

She would have fallen asleep, but there was a question at the edge of her mind. And because she had come to feel comfortable with Laszlo, Ingrid allowed herself to ask, "Laszlo, why doesn't my grandmother like my mother?"

Laszlo was visibly alarmed by the question. He stopped the car, made a few signs of distress, and stepped outside.

"You must not," said Laszlo, after Ingrid had hit him, "the young countess must not mention her mother. It would be most unfortunate for the young countess to mention her mother, Krysztina, before the countess, her grandmother."

Rather sensibly, Ingrid asked, "Why?"

"The young countess must not ask why," said Laszlo. "Did your father, the count, not tell you often of their misfortune?"

"No," said Ingrid.

"Most unfortunate," said Laszlo. "Most unfortunate."

Laszlo had stopped beside a field of broom. Between the car and the bright yellow weeds, there was a watery ditch in which there were small eels.

Laszlo touched Ingrid's shoulder.

"The young countess must tell no one I have spoken of this," he said. "The young countess' mother and father are related. They are distant cousins. . . . The Countess Nadja, God keep her soul, had many relatives because there once were many Balazses in Puffdorf. But only one part of the Balazses were given Castle Puffdorf. . . . The other Balazses were very jealous and unhappy, and the family split in two and no one from one side has spoken to anyone from the other side since the eighteenth century. The young countess' mother is from the wrong Balazses."

"The wrong Balazses? Why are they the wrong Balazses?"

"Oh, the young countess must know that whoever is not noble born is wrong."

"But Nadja wasn't a noblewoman," declared Ingrid.

"That is true," said Laszlo, "but she became a noble-woman, and all of her descendants are noble. The young countess herself is, perhaps, noble. You are the first Balazs, since the eighteenth century, who has blood from both sides of the Balazses, you see? No one knows if you are noble or not. The Countess Liliane has sent for you, to see if you will overcome your trials and prove yourself noble. For my part, I am certain the young countess will overcome them all."

"What trials?" asked Ingrid.

Laszlo bowed. "That is all I may say," he said. "And I beg the young countess to tell no one I have said so much. I would certainly be punished."

"I won't tell," said Ingrid.

"The young countess is as kind as her father," said Laszlo.

They returned to the limousine, and Laszlo drove on to Liliana.

He had given Ingrid something to think about, though. She wondered if she was noble and what, exactly, "noble" meant.

As Ingrid wondered about her nobility, they passed through Liliana, a small town, and took a winding dirt road to another winding dirt road, at the side of which Ingrid saw a deer. They then drove up a hill, at the top of which was a magnificent, massive, tree-dwarfing mansion. In front of the mansion was a drinking well beneath an olive tree. And in the lower branches of the olive tree there were white roses.

It was, to say the least, astounding. Here, before her, was the real version of a drawing she'd made, a picture come to life. No wonder her parents had been amazed.

Laszlo opened Ingrid's door.

The wooden door to the mansion opened and a thin old woman, her crown of white hair stiff as a helmet, stepped out.

The first thing she did, once she reached the limousine, was to hit Laszlo on the back with her thin silver cane and ask, "I trust everything went well?"

Laszlo winced, but said, "It was wonderful, Countess. Countess Ingrid is just like her father. . . ."

Countess Liliane struck Laszlo once again. "That's enough, Laszlo. I shall speak to Ingrid myself."

She looked at her granddaughter, then said, "Before you go, Laszlo, please take the young countess' dress for her, and burn it with the refuse."

"I don't have anything else to wear," said Ingrid.

Her grandmother looked at her closely for a few moments. "I would rather see you naked than in such rags," she said. "Besides, I have brought this for you."

She put her cane under her arm, clapped her hands, and three young women came from the house. One brought three white bedsheets, another a long blue silk dress, and the third a pair of black shoes.

Ingrid hesitated. She found it annoying to be told what to wear, but after all . . . she had brought nothing but a toothbrush and her passport. She would have to change sooner or later. And then, perhaps it was customary, in the Old Country, to burn old clothes. And then again, the dress was lovely: robin's egg blue.

The three young women held the sheets up around her while Ingrid changed from her pinching dress to the soft silk one, while Ingrid took off her shoes and put on the new ones. Everything fit her perfectly.

"It all fits," said Ingrid.

"Of course it fits," said her grandmother. "Those are some of the very clothes I wore when I was your age. You are my granddaughter, after all."

And, in fact, in the face of Liliane Montesquieu von Puffdorf di Turbino de la Louve des Balazs, Ingrid recognized the face of her own father.

12

Manners

ountess Liliane looked at her granddaughter and, not unkindly, said, "Come with me, child." The countess walked into her mansion, leaving Ingrid to follow.

If the mansion was impressive from the outside, it was intimidating from within. Ingrid was not used to her new shoes and the blue silk dress, which, at every step, sounded like willows in a windstorm, but the mansion was so immense and there were so many hallways leading to other hallways that, if she had not kept up with her grandmother, she might easily have gotten lost somewhere between the front door and the dining room.

The dining room, when they came to it, was remarkably simple. It was a long white room in which there was a long oak table. A single narrow window looked out onto a courtyard, in which there was a marble statue of a lamb. The ceiling was high and from the ceiling there dangled two wrought-iron chandeliers, which held twelve candles each.

Though the table was long and wide enough to fit twenty-four people, there was only one plate upon it.

"Sit," said the countess, and Ingrid, pulling her dress into place behind her, sat at the table.

"Please eat," said the countess, and Ingrid would have begun eating immediately, as she was hungry, but . . . on the wide white plate before her, there was a single meager sardine.

On the table, to the left of the plate, there were five forks: every fork a different size, one as large as Ingrid's hand, one as small as her thumb.

On the table, to the right of the plate, there were five knives: each knife a different size, one as long as Ingrid's forearm, another as thin and short as her baby finger.

On the table, above the plate, there were two spoons lying on a bright crimson napkin. . . .

Though she was well behaved and had wonderful table manners, the only thing Ingrid knew how to use for certain was the napkin. So she put the napkin on her lap, picked the sardine up with her fingers, and ate it.

The countess stared at her granddaughter for a cold moment, then sternly said, "Why did you use your fingers, child?"

"I couldn't find the proper knife and fork," said Ingrid.

"You are right," said Countess Liliane. "The table has not been properly set."

Countess Liliane smiled, bowed her head, and clapped her hands together. Into the room rushed two short men, both dressed in black suits, both with their heads bowed.

"Please bring the rest of the young countess' meal," said Countess Liliane, "and have the maids bring the rest of the cutlery."

As if they had been waiting for the countess' signal, three young women came into the dining room. All three wore such stiff clothes, it seemed to Ingrid they were dressed in white papier-mâché.

The first woman carried a copper tray on which there were silver knives and forks. The second carried a silver tray on which there were six porcelain bowls: wild rice, whipped parsnips, candied sweet potatoes, carrots in raspberry sauce, roast potatoes, and buttered asparagus. And the third brought a large porcelain tray on which there was a single, magnificent roast turkey.

One of the men served Ingrid a small portion of each dish.

The turkey was not simply turkey. It was a turkey in which there was a whole chicken, in which there was a whole pheasant, in which there was a whole pigeon, in which there was a thrush, in which there was a hummingbird, in which there was a candied fly.

Before Ingrid could begin eating, the Countess Liliane offered her a plate on which there was a fist of dark, almost black, bread. "I am pleased your father has raised you properly," she said. "You have earned the right to eat this."

"What is it?" asked Ingrid.

"It is our bread," she answered. "The Balazses have eaten pumpernickel for centuries."

It tasted like a mouthful of wet earth.

When Ingrid had finished the bread, the Countess Liliane smiled and said, "Now, please eat."

And, because she was polite, Ingrid ate everything she was served. Even the fly, which, though hard as a tiny leather button, tasted of maple sugar. What's more, Ingrid used every one of the knives and forks she had been given.

She would have used the spoons for her dessert but she fell asleep, sitting straight up, before the persimmon ice cream could be brought out.

13

A Curious Book

The next morning, Ingrid woke in a bed as wide and as long as her room at home. The bed was soft and warm, but she was startled when, looking out a window, she saw a green and hilly world, not the city she expected.

There was a brief, vigorous knock at her door. Then, without waiting for a response, Countess Liliane stepped into Ingrid's bedroom. "Good morning, Ingrid. It is time you were awake."

Her grandmother was not as brusque as she'd been the day before, but she was brisk. "I have arranged for you to have a bath in your bedroom," she said.

And before Ingrid could object, two tall men brought in a large copper bathtub. They were followed by two women who poured hot or cold water into the tub, until it was just the temperature Ingrid wanted. The women held sheets up around the tub as Ingrid bathed.

As she was bathing, her grandmother asked, almost casually, "I wonder, child, if you have had strange dreams?"

The countess spoke in such a peculiar way, Ingrid wasn't certain how to answer. Still, it occurred to her that it was now Monday morning, and that for the first Sunday night in months she had not dreamed of wolves, forks, or bread.

"I used to dream about a wolf. . . ."

The countess was pleased by her answer. "How interesting," she said. "But we will speak of all this later. You must finish bathing."

How annoying it was to be told to bathe, then to hurry up bathing.

"Did my mother dream about wolves?" Ingrid asked.

There was a silence.

The women holding her sheets up stiffened. Her grandmother's face appeared above the sheets.

"Your mother," said the countess, "is not noble. She is not a proper Balazs. You will not speak of her in my presence."

Ingrid was a polite girl, but she loved her mother fiercely. She would have defied a thousand Lilianes to defend her.

"She's my mother," said Ingrid. "I can talk about her when I want."

Countess Liliane, her face pink with outrage, did not know what to say. She was not used to contradiction, and she was too old to remember a time when she was not sovereign. But she recognized in Ingrid's tone, in the rightness of what Ingrid said, something that reminded her of herself.

"Very well," said Countess Liliane. "You may speak of your mother when you like, but I ask you to do so out of my hearing. The thought of your mother causes me pain. Please finish bathing. I will see to breakfast. Do you prefer smoked eel or poached partridge eggs? Not to worry. We will have both."

With that, Countess Liliane withdrew from Ingrid's room.

Though she was still annoyed, Ingrid finished bathing while trying to decide which was better: partridge eggs or eel? Neither sounded appealing.

As it happened, the eel and the partridge eggs were both delicious. The eel was particularly surprising. It had been smoked whole, and its rather long body lay on a rather long silver platter. Its head, with its curved white teeth, was unpleasant to see, but the eel tasted of salted fish and a distant forest fire.

When they had finished eating, the Countess Liliane snapped her fingers to get Ingrid's attention.

"My dear girl," she said, "we have much to discuss. I should very much like to answer all your questions, but I'm afraid I will be indisposed for the next few days. You will see very little of me. Of course, you may ask Laszlo, or any of the servants, for whatever you like. Do you see?"

"Yes," said Ingrid. But she was disappointed because she still hoped to befriend her grandmother.

"In the meantime," continued the countess, "you must feel free to wander the grounds. There is a pool in the olive grove. You may swim, if you do not drown. And there are peach trees and cherry trees. I enjoyed walking in the orchards when I was younger, as did your father. And then, of course, there is the mansion. You may explore it as you like. Almost every room has something to recommend it. Especially the library. I believe you would find the library most interesting. There is, however, one place you must not go and that is underground. The dungeon is forbidden to young children and I would be most unhappy were you to go downstairs without my permission. Do you understand?"

"Yes," said Ingrid. Though she wondered why the countess thought this would be difficult to understand, and wondered as well what *was* underground.

"Good," said the countess. "Then I will leave you to your own resources, for a few days. We will discuss everything when I return. You will see, child. Time will pass quickly."

The time passed quickly indeed.

Ingrid was used to being alone, but unused to such interesting surroundings. At first, she did much as her grandmother suggested. She walked in the orchards, eating peaches or cherries. She sat beneath the boughs of the trees, or walked in the gardens. She swam in the cold water of the pool. But the days were so hot she spent most of her time indoors, away from the sun.

Sadly, there was no one to talk to, indoors. Or no one who wished to talk.

Everyone was suddenly (and suspiciously) busy, whenever Ingrid passed. A butler, who seemed to be doing nothing as she approached, would turn to a wall and wipe it vigorously with a kerchief. Even Laszlo seemed too busy to talk. He was always in the same place (the kitchen), and always doing the same thing (plucking chickens). He would smile and bow and, if he spoke at all, politely advise Ingrid to spend time in the library.

And so, Ingrid explored the mansion.

It was, as her grandmother suggested, a fascinating place. In one room, she found a golden needle and a spool of delicate, gold thread. In another, there was a closet filled with silver dresses and red shoes. One room was a theater, with seats and a stage; another was a pool filled with cool water. There were magnificent paintings, in some rooms. In others, there were clay statues of sheep, wooden statues of the Virgin Mary, bronze statues of spindly spiders.

In the room she liked best, there were two pianos, a harpsichord, and a violin.

Ingrid might have gone on exploring for months. There seemed to be no end of rooms and unexpected delights. But two things happened to stop her exploration.

First, more curious than defiant, she went secretly, quietly, down the staircase that led underground. She might even have reached the dungeon but, as if he'd been expecting her, Laszlo (whom, moments before, she'd seen in the kitchen) met her at the bottom of the steps. He bowed politely and, once she'd hit him with the stick he offered, politely said, "The young countess has surely lost her way. In my opinion, it would be unwise for her to continue."

Caught out, Ingrid said, "I'm sorry, Laszlo."

"The young countess need not apologize," said Laszlo. "Her intentions are spotless, I am certain of it."

They then walked up the stairs together, slowly so Laszlo could keep up.

After that, Ingrid was too embarrassed to think of going to the dungeon on her own and too embarrassed to do any more delving. Fortunately, it was shortly after her venture downstairs that the second thing happened: Ingrid discovered the library.

It was not the usual library, filled with encyclopedias and old tomes. It was a room, two stories high, stuffed with an astounding variety of books in a variety of languages. And most of the books Ingrid touched were interesting in their own way, even those in languages she did not know. For instance, there was a book, written in what looked like Chinese, with vivid pictures of the moon, some of which glowed with a pale light that filled the library with nighttime. Another book, in no language Ingrid knew, seemed to be a history of water. It had a thousand drawings of water but, most interesting, there was a secret hollow in its pages and, in the hollow, a large blue pearl.

There were books bound in fur, in feathers, in soft skin. There was a book as tall as Ingrid (a short story by Dumas) and a book the size of her thumb (an encyclopedia). It was endlessly diverting.

For days, Ingrid did little but climb up and down ladders, reaching for books that looked interesting. She read some of those she found in English but, really, the exciting part was the search. How wonderful to find a book that said the word "Ruth," when it was opened, and another that spoke the words, "Here I am."

Then, quite by accident, on one of the lower shelves, Ingrid found a modest, pale green book called *A History of the Balazses: 1711 to the Future*. She didn't think much of the *History* when she pulled it from the shelf. It looked dull. Still, she thought it might be pleasant to read about Nadja, about her own family.

It was wonderful. She read all about Nadja: her childhood in Puffdorf, her encounter with the wolves, her marriage to Antonio, the count of Turbino. And she was going to read about the agreement Nadja had reached with the wolves, when . . . she suddenly wondered if there was a chapter in the book about her grandmother.

There was. It was called "Countess Liliane and the Long Silence." And was there one about her father? Yes, there was a chapter about her father as well. It was called "Sandor Ignatz Count Balazs in the New World." And was there one about her? Oh, yes, there certainly was, though it had the mysterious title "Ingrid Countess Balazs and the End of Gabor."

Why would anyone have written about her?

Yet there it was, a whole chapter to herself: the story of her birth, her schooling at Queen Elizabeth, the poverty her parents had chosen, her journey to the Old World. . . .

Ingrid read every word, until she reached a page that began:

Then, quite by accident, on one of the lower shelves, Ingrid found a modest, pale green book called A History of the Balazses: 1711 to the Future.

No sooner did she read these words than the book turned to salt and ran through her fingers, leaving a heap of white dust on the floor.

14

A Simple Task

Ingrid was frightened when her book turned to salt. She was then startled when, moments later, as if she'd been waiting for just this instant, her grandmother entered the library.

"My dear, dear girl," said Countess Liliane, "you have found our history." She put her arms around Ingrid and held her so close that Ingrid could feel how thin her grandmother was, could smell her lavender perfume.

"But the book turned to salt," said Ingrid. "Is it magic?"

"Yes, my dear, it is a sort of magic. It is a book found only once a generation and only by a Balazs. It is a terrifying book. But, please, let us talk no more about it. You have shown your impeccable manners. You have found the secret history of our family. There is only one trial left for you to overcome."

The Countess Liliane put her arm around Ingrid's shoulder, kissed her temple, and led her gently from the library.

"When you return from the labyrinth," she said, "you will truly be my granddaughter. And all I have will be yours."

It was a lot to understand at once.

Ingrid had found a book that turned to salt and, then, her grandmother had kissed her temple and told her that everything she had seen, the grounds she'd explored, the books she'd read . . . all of it would belong to her when she returned from the labyrinth. The labyrinth? That was a maze, wasn't it? What kind of maze would it be?

It was all so astounding, Ingrid did not know if she should be happy or alarmed.

That evening, they ate an enormous meal. There were dishes of spiced deer, roast goose, braised brisket, stewed bear, and jugged hare. There were bowls of whipped turnip, zucchini flowers, thrice mashed potatoes, wild rice, and cherry soup. There was cucumber salad, shredded carrots with stewed gooseberries, red cabbage with . . .

"You must eat as much as you are able," said Countess Liliane.

Quite sensibly, Ingrid asked why.

"I may not say," answered the countess, "but tomorrow you will understand."

Was there anything more mysterious than this "I may not say"? It seemed to Ingrid that, from the moment she'd first heard about Countess Liliane, there were things about which she could get no clear answer. There was always *something* that couldn't be said, *something* that had to be mentioned later, *something* she would understand in a while, in a day, *sometime*.

As if she knew Ingrid's thoughts, her grandmother said, "You have my word, child. When you return from the labyrinth, I will answer every one of your questions."

The countess smiled slightly and clapped her hands together and in came still more food, enough to feed Ingrid, Ingrid, Ingrid, and Ingrid.

The following morning, at breakfast, there was almost as much to eat as there had been the night before. There was herring, kippers, smoked haddock, boiled eel, two sorts of egg, three kinds of bacon, four types of bread, and five varieties of cereal with cow's milk.

It was as if someone thought Ingrid would never eat again.

"Please, child, take as much as you are able," said Countess Liliane.

But Ingrid ate sparingly because she was not hungry, and because she disliked feeling full, and because this was the morning she would go to the labyrinth. She was excited and nervous, because she did not know what was expected of her, or how difficult the labyrinth was to get through, or why she needed to go at all.

With these thoughts in mind, it was not easy to eat.

When she had taken all she would, her grandmother asked, "Have you written to your father, child?"

"Yes," said Ingrid.

Actually, she had written her parents almost every evening, sending her letters off with a butler before going to sleep.

Her grandmother smiled, then sighed as if she was tired. "You must make yourself ready," said the countess. "Please wait in your room. Laszlo will come for you presently."

For Ingrid, in her room, every moment passed slowly. It felt almost as if they had forgotten her, and then . . . there was a knock at the door, and Laszlo entered.

"The young countess must wear this dress," he said kindly. "And no shoes."

He gave her a short-sleeved silk umber dress and,

when she had changed, he led her to the stone staircase that spiraled downward.

At the very bottom of the steps, Countess Liliane was waiting for them in a dark and empty room. She held a lantern, in which there was a copper-colored beeswax candle, and she stood before two large wooden doors, one a foot from the other.

"Do you know," she said, "it seems not so long ago that I stood where you are and I passed through the door. My own father was with me, then. A wonderful man. I wish you had met him." The Countess seemed slightly amused. "You remind me of him," she said. Then: "You are a Balazs. I *do* feel this."

She put a hand on Ingrid's shoulder, and gave her the lantern.

"You must," she said, "go in this door, on the left, and leave by that door, there. Once you go in, this door will be locked, and that will be the only way out. Do you understand?"

Yes, she understood and, what's more, there was so little distance between the doors, Ingrid was certain it would take no more than a little while. The labyrinth could not be vast. It made her wonder why her grandmother and Laszlo were looking at her with such concern.

"Yes," said Ingrid. "I understand."

"Then, may God keep you safe," said the countess.

15

In the Labyrinth

Once the door closed behind her, and she heard it being locked, Ingrid found herself in a dark corridor. There was a candle in a sconce on the wall: a tall candle. It was the only source of light besides her lantern. The rest of the corridor was bible black.

What a strange corridor it was.

Ingrid looked for a way to turn right, in the direction of the door she was supposed to reach, but . . . there was no way to go right.

Finally, after she had walked for five minutes or so, she came to three dark doors. Ingrid would not have known they were doors but for the three brass door-knobs that glinted in the lantern light.

The doors didn't lead in the direction she wanted, but Ingrid decided to open them anyway.

The first door opened onto a long tall room. Up near the ceiling, there were two small circular windows through which a pale light shone. The room was empty, except for a wire cage in which there was a square loaf of black bread.

What a strange thing to have in a room, Ingrid thought. And, thinking she might need something to eat later, she opened the cage and took the bread with her.

The second door opened onto a large square room, lit by four tall candles. In the center of this room, there was a medium-sized cage. In the cage was an immense black bird on a wooden stool.

Ingrid thought it very cruel to leave the bird in such a sad place, but she really didn't know what to do with a large bird, nor how to take care of it. So, she was about to leave when the bird looked up at her and said, in perfect English, "Do you suppose I could have a piece of bread?"

Ingrid was so surprised, she laughed. This was just like the bear she had seen in Lukacs, she thought, but here the man (or small child, perhaps) was dressed as a crow.

"What are you doing here?" she asked.

The crow stared at her and repeated, in perfect English, "Do you suppose I could have a piece of bread?"

Ingrid tried in every way she could to start a conversation. She asked the bird its name, she asked where it lived, she asked why it would not talk to her. But to all her questions, the crow simply requested a piece of her bread, politely but in a tone that annoyed her.

Ingrid left without giving the bird a crumb. She was annoyed, it's true, but there was something else . . . something about bread.

The third door opened onto a room that was filled with darkness: darkness like burying your face in a black cloth. Ingrid held the lantern before her, but in this room the light would not carry. She could see nothing but the candle flame, which, in the darkness, looked like a piece of sharp red glass. There was nothing in this room for her.

Ingrid walked further and further along the corridor. It curved slightly left, then curved sharply left, then curved again and came to a fork.

The corridor went off in two directions: two corridors. She would have to choose a way. She tilted her lantern into the corridor on the right: nothing but more corridor and darkness. And she would have looked down the left corridor too, except that . . . as she put her lantern into the corridor, a strong draft blew out the candle and Ingrid was left in total darkness.

16

Gabor

It might have been worse.

Ingrid might have been left in the terrifying dark, with no idea where to turn. As it was, she was in the terrifying dark, frightened but . . . she immediately thought of the room with the birdcage. There had been four candles there.

It was just a matter of staying calm, though she could not see her own hand before her, keeping to the wall on the left until she came to the proper doorknob, which she would feel, even if she couldn't see it.

Well, it's easy enough to say "walk in the dark," but it's not so easy to do when you're frightened. The corridor was quiet. There was only the sound of her feet on the stone floor. She kept her back to the wall and went slowly back the way she'd come until, yes, there it was, the first doorknob, which would have been the third one, the one that went into the dark room. She went on to the second doorknob, the room that held the birdcage.

Ingrid turned the brass knob and opened the door. She could see into the lighted room but . . .

"What can I do for you?"

The same crow she'd seen in the cage now flew directly above her. It spoke politely but, out of the cage, blocking her way, it seemed as tall as Ingrid and she was, a little, intimidated.

"Please," she said. "My candle blew out. I need another one."

"Ah," said the crow. "You need a candle. A while ago I needed bread. . . ."

"Yes," said Ingrid, "but you were not polite."

"I was most polite," said the crow. "You ignored me."

"I didn't ignore you. I tried to talk to you, but you wouldn't answer me, and –"

"It's all history now," said the bird. "I don't like you or your company."

"But . . . ," said Ingrid.

The bird swooped down at her, its claws extended, its wings flapping as it cawed angrily. As quickly as she could, Ingrid ran from the room and pulled the door closed behind her.

She knocked at the door. She called out, "Please, I need a candle, please. I'm very sorry if I upset you. Would you like a piece of bread?"

All to no use. She heard the bird's hoarse caw and its fitfully fluttering wings. It would not let her in.

Now here was a predicament. Ingrid was still alone in the dark. She could not go forward to find the door that led out of the maze. She could only go back, back to the door through which she'd entered. There had been a candle at the door and . . . perhaps her grandmother was waiting there. Ingrid could ask for another lantern and return to her task.

Yes. She would have to go back. And back she went, feeling her way in the dark, keeping to the wall, but . . . after what seemed forever, she was not at the door. She went back and back, in the direction from which she'd come, but the corridor seemed to stretch on and on. There was no sign of the door, no candlelight, and Ingrid was well and truly lost.

She called out, "Is there anyone there? Can anyone hear me?" Her voice carried, then echoed, then died.

It was then, lost in darkness, with no apparent means out, that she began to cry. It seemed wicked that her grandmother had abandoned her in this terrifying darkness.

While she had hope of getting light from the bird's room, she had confidence. Now, she was unsure what to do, how to go on. It even occurred to her that she was not a true Balazs, that she would not – what was the word? – survive.

Just think . . . days ago she'd been at home in (wonderful) Toronto, with her parents whom she had never loved as deeply as she did at this moment. What would her father do, if he were here? Indeed, what had he done, when he was in the labyrinth? He seemed, to Ingrid, so confident and strong, she could not imagine him upset.

The thought of her father was such a comfort, she stopped crying. There were now so many questions to ask him, from *Were you frightened?* to *How did you get out?*

Perhaps because of her sniffles, Ingrid did not hear the approach of someone carrying a torch. She saw the light before she realized what it was: a long bright torch in the mouth of a wolf. The wolf, on all fours, carried the torch very carefully indeed: its flame was as far from the wolf's muzzle as could be.

Ingrid barely had time to be either amazed or frightened. The wolf approached, holding the torch so that Ingrid could take it from his jaws. Ingrid lit the lantern and she put the torch in a niche on the wall. She was neither amazed nor frightened, but she could not think of a single word to say.

"You are welcome," said the wolf.

As politely as she could, Ingrid said, "I'm so sorry. Thank you. . . ."

"Gabor," said the wolf.

"Thank you, Gabor."

"And your name is?"

"Ingrid."

"Just Ingrid?"

"Ingrid Balazs."

"Oh, I don't think so," said Gabor. "I have never spoken to anyone with a name so short."

Ingrid sighed. "Ingrid Montesquieu von Puffdorf di Turbino de la Louve des Balazs," she said.

"I thought so," said Gabor. "You are the countess."

"No," said Ingrid, "my grandmother is the countess."

"Your grandmother? She is not much of a countess, if you ask me. She's selfish and she does not keep her word."

"Do you know her well?"

"I wouldn't say I know her well, but I met her when she was just about your age. How old are you, if you don't mind my asking?"

"I'm eleven," said Ingrid.

"Well, there you are," said the wolf. "I met her when she was exactly your age, and I haven't seen her since. But she was a most unpleasant eleven-year-old. I don't see how she could have improved. The seed holds the tree, in my opinion. Still, I do not mean to insult your grandmother. Perhaps she has found goodwill."

And Gabor bowed.

It was an unusual sight. He pushed his front paws forward as far as they would go, made a bowl of his back, then lifted his head before lowering it again.

Ingrid was, as you might expect, bewildered. She was in a dark corridor with a wolf that spoke the most beautiful English, a wolf that seemed polite.

"I'm sorry, Countess. May I do something for you?"

"Oh," said Ingrid, "do you know the way out of here?"

"I do," said Gabor, "and I will happily take you. I must say, you seem different from most of the others who've been here. You don't seem at all selfish."

He looked at her intently, as if waiting for an answer, but for the life of her Ingrid could not decide what his question had been. She thought for a moment before she said, "Everyone is a little selfish, I think. I know I am, though I shouldn't be. I wish I weren't selfish."

"No, no, Countess. You must never wish that. You must wish to know *when* to be selfish. That is more reasonable, in my opinion. There, you see? You really are quite different. Let us walk. I will show you the way."

17

Gabor and Ingrid

I t was a little disorienting.

No, it was more than a little disorienting. Ingrid was, as she walked through the corridor, confused and wary. There were a number of things that contributed to her wariness: the darkness, only slightly dissipated by the lantern, which she'd lit with Gabor's torch; the strangeness of speaking to a man in a wolf suit (it had to be a man – didn't it? – he spoke English as well as she did); the peculiarity of speaking to Gabor as he walked behind her. . . .

(How uncomfortable it must be, walking on all fours.)

Gabor refused to walk in front of Ingrid. He stayed behind her, but sometimes his head was so close to her elbow that she felt the prickles of his fur.

"Why don't you walk in front?" she'd asked.

"No, Countess, I cannot. For one thing, I haven't the lantern. For another, I prefer to guide rather than lead. It is my nature, you see. You mustn't be afraid."

A very obscure answer, it seemed to Ingrid.

"Is it far?" she asked.

"Not far if you know the way," said Gabor, "but it takes time. If I were alone, I could do it in an hour or so. It will take a little longer, with you."

They came to the three doors.

"I've been in these rooms," said Ingrid.

"I'm sure you have," Gabor answered, "but perhaps you didn't know there was a door at the other end of this one?"

Gabor went to the third door and Ingrid opened it.

"It's so much easier to open doors with hands, isn't it, Countess? Otherwise I would open them for you."

They walked through the darkness and, yes, at the far end, there was indeed another door. They walked through it and they found themselves in another corridor.

They walked along this corridor and came to three doors, visible mostly by their brass knobs.

"Are these three rooms like the first three?" asked Ingrid.

"Not exactly," said Gabor.

Ingrid opened the first door. Here there was a cage, with its loaf of bread, and four candles. In the second room, they were in total darkness, but in the darkness there was a bird in a cage. It fluttered its wings as Ingrid held the torch up before it, but otherwise it kept still. In the third room there were high windows for light, and at the very back there was a door.

"The door in this room leads nowhere," said Gabor.

Ingrid and Gabor continued along the corridor for a time and then, after taking the left side of the fork, came to a door that, in turn, led to another long corridor with three doors.

After this, they came to another corridor, and then another, and then another. . . .

It was intriguing, in a way, so many slight variations. Every one of the corridors had three doors, and behind one of the doors there would be a window, a loaf of bread, a crow, candles, a door, or darkness. But it was never the same way twice: sometimes there was a crow and candles, sometimes a crow and darkness, sometimes a crow and high windows, sometimes a crow and a door . . . and sometimes the doors they found led out, sometimes they led nowhere.

Really, it was not like being in a dream – it was like being in a fever. No wonder it took so long to leave. Were it not for Gabor, Ingrid might have been lost for days, for weeks, for . . .

"Gabor"

"Yes, Countess?"

"Has anyone been really lost in here?"

"Yes, Countess. Thirty-three people have died here."

"How did they die?"

"Most of them died as you might have died, if I hadn't found you. If you walk too far in the first corridor, you will fall into the buried lake and drown."

"I might have drowned?"

"Yes, but no, Countess. None of your family has ever died here. I could feel your presence as soon as you entered. I must say, you seemed most brave. I admired you straightaway. I would have come sooner, but I was several corridors away."

"How do you know your way so well, in here?"

"It is my home, Countess."

(It was becoming more difficult to believe Gabor's words. It didn't seem possible that anyone should live in such darkness.)

"How did the others die?" asked Ingrid.

"It is most unpleasant to speak of, Countess, but I myself dispatched them. I have eaten two or three people."

A shiver ran along Ingrid's spine. It was almost as if Gabor were telling the truth, it really was. But she did not believe him. He seemed too kind to have thought of eating anyone.

"Why did you eat them?"

"They were not supposed to be down here and they wished me harm."

They walked on, opening the door to a room in which there were high windows and a door that led to another room. It was difficult for Ingrid to keep herself from turning to look at Gabor when he spoke.

Though she was still a little frightened of him, she was grateful for Gabor's company. He made her feel as if this walk through the maze were an innocent thing.

And then . . .

"Countess," said Gabor, "I'm feeling quite hungry. I wonder if I might have some of your bread?"

It was a strange moment. As he spoke, Ingrid felt as if she were in a dream, not just any dream but the dream she had last had a week before, the dream in which she'd given bread to a wolf.

And so, she thought, I wasn't dreaming.

And what was it her father had told her?

Ingrid, you mustn't give bread to the wolf.

Why not? she wondered.

"I'm sorry, Gabor, but this bread is not for you."

"I really am quite hungry, Countess. It is difficult for me to open small cages. I cannot remember when it was I last ate bread."

"I'm sorry, Gabor, but I can't give you any."

"Why can't you, Countess?"

Now that was a difficult question.

"Because," said Ingrid, "it's not good enough for you."

Gabor growled as he said, "And yet the countess will eat it?"

"No, Gabor. I'm only bringing it for emergencies."

Gabor bowed. "The countess is noble and good," he said. "We will see she does not starve."

And they walked on.

It was all most peculiar. If Ingrid didn't know better, she'd have sworn it was a wolf she was speaking to, not a man, but no wolf could have been so human.

After they'd gone on for a while in silence, Ingrid asked, "Gabor, what do you usually eat?"

"The countess must know what I eat, or she could not have known I do not eat bread. Still, from time to time, Countess, I tire of eating mice. I have been eating mice for centuries."

"Haven't you eaten anything else?"

"Well," said Gabor thoughtfully, "nothing but an occasional crow."

"Have you really eaten people?"

"I have eaten a few, but I must confess I do not enjoy the taste." Gabor sounded slightly disgusted, but then his voice softened. "I should not like to eat you, Countess. I am pleased you are a Balazs."

18

Gabor's Beard

As they walked, Gabor and Ingrid spoke of more pleasant things. He asked about her life before coming to the labyrinth. And Ingrid told him everything: about her parents, their life in Toronto, the letter from her grandmother, her flight to Budapest, her drive in the Old Country and the things she'd seen.

"I liked your father," said Gabor. "He disappointed me, but perhaps there was a reason. Your grandmother, on the other hand, I did not like your grandmother at all."

"When did you meet my father?"

"When he was your age."

"That was a very long time ago," said Ingrid.

"Yes," said Gabor, "but I wonder how much he has changed. He was a good companion . . . very much like yourself, Countess."

"He *is* a good companion," said Ingrid.

"There you are, then," said Gabor. "I wonder how much people change. The young countess' father was born good, and he is good still. Just as, almost certainly, the young countess was born noble and nobly she will live. I cannot imagine the Countess Ingrid speaking ill of someone who did not deserve it, or breaking her word, or . . . ah, we have arrived. Here is the door out."

And, yes, there it was: a door identical to all the other doors, at the end of a passage that was identical to all the other passages, save that here, as at the entrance, there was a torch in a sconce. It was, when you thought about it, incredible that anyone should find their way through on their own. Without Gabor, she would have wandered forever.

Ingrid turned to thank the wolf. She held the lantern up and . . . maybe it was the light, maybe the way she held the lantern, but Gabor's face was strangely lit. It looked as if a wolf's head were floating in the darkness: its eyes a yellow-green, its ears cocked, its muzzle white and tawny, and its fur so vivid Ingrid thought she could have counted every strand if she'd wanted.

It was as beautiful a face as Ingrid had ever seen. Now that she had reached her destination, wasn't it time for Gabor to take his mask off?

"Your mask is beautiful," she said. And she pulled at the white fur she thought of as Gabor's beard.

Now, this was a grave mistake. Gabor stood up on his hind legs and howled in indignation. He knocked the lantern from Ingrid's hand so that two of its panes broke and its candle guttered out. He growled as if he would eat her on the spot.

Terrified, Ingrid turned towards the door. But before she could move, Gabor knocked her down and stood over her, one paw on her chest.

"I'm so sorry," said Ingrid. "I'm so sorry. I thought it was a mask."

For a moment, the labyrinth was quiet, save for the sound of Ingrid's breathing and Gabor's rumbling growl. Then, as if he were embarrassed, Gabor retreated.

"I am sorry, Countess, very sorry, but it is most painful to have my fur pulled as you did. It is how my mother punished me, when I was a cub. Most painful, but . . . I am puzzled. No true Balazs has pulled the fur beneath my teeth, but none has been as kind as you, either. So, I will be merciful. I release you, as I have released all the Balazses before you, and I ask of you the same thing I have asked of all: will you return to the labyrinth and stay with me?" Gabor bowed. "Will you?"

Ingrid was rattled, it's true, but there was such sadness in the wolf's tone, she said yes without thinking.

"So you have made a promise," said Gabor. "Then, I will look for you tomorrow."

He politely pushed the lantern her way, then bowed, when, before leaving, Ingrid looked back at him.

"None of the Balazses has kept his promise," said Gabor. "None has ever returned. I have been so often disappointed, I wonder if I shall ever know any world but this one. But you are different, Countess. I will allow myself to hope for your return."

With that, the wolf retreated to the darkness.

19

Ingrid's Return

When Ingrid stepped out of the labyrinth, it was as if she walked into a new world. Not only because the room she entered was filled with light, but also because it was bursting with red lilies and white carnations, hundreds of them. They were everywhere, and in the middle of this room of flowers Laszlo sat in a wooden chair, asleep, his head drooping as if it were a sunflower.

When he heard the door to the labyrinth open, Laszlo jumped up and ran from the room. He wasn't gone a minute before he returned with a stick and a glass of water. The stick was for his back, of course, and when he could speak he said, "Forgive me, Countess," and drank the water himself. "Forgive me, but we did not expect the countess to return so soon. It has never happened. The countess, your grandmother, is not here to greet you, but I have had her summoned. She will be here. . . ."

He had no sooner said the words "She will be here" than Ingrid heard her grandmother's voice.

"Laszlo, I warned you not to disturb me before my granddaughter's return. If you do not have significant news, I will have you punished for dirtying my sleep. I —"

The countess stopped as soon as she saw Ingrid. "My dear?" she said finally.

And Ingrid ran to her grandmother and cried in her arms.

"Laszlo," said the countess, "leave us."

When Laszlo had gone, Countess Liliane said, "But why are you crying, child? You are a true Balazs. And you have done something no other Balazs has ever done. You have been in the labyrinth for two hours. No one has done this in fewer than eight. You should be proud."

"I promised to go back," said Ingrid. "I have to go back tomorrow."

Countess Liliane smiled. "We have all made this promise," she said. "We have all been invited to return, but it is forbidden. Those who come out of the maze must never go back. They remain here and take up what belongs to them by right. You have been brave. You have proved yourself a Balazs. There is no more for you to do."

Ingrid's grandmother, a forbidding woman only a short while ago, was now kindness itself.

"But I promised," said Ingrid. "I have to tell my parents what happened."

"My dear," said Countess Liliane, "your father also wanted to return. He was most upset when I refused to allow him back into the labyrinth. But one simply cannot allow a Balazs to live underground, and with such a dangerous animal." She touched Ingrid's hair, and asked, "What did the wolf say his name was?"

"Gabor," said Ingrid.

"Ah," said Countess Liliane, "he was Istvan when I met him, and he was Gregor to your father."

"But he's the same wolf?"

"Yes, and he has a hundred names. Did he speak to you in Hungarian?"

"No, he speaks English," said Ingrid.

"He speaks the language of the one who enters. With you, he spoke English. I am sorry the preparations for your return have not been finished. Let us find you some chocolate. Come with me. Laszlo! Bring the chocolate, please. Countess Ingrid has returned from the labyrinth."

As they walked up to Ingrid's room, she saw there were flowers everywhere, as if spring had come to the inside of the mansion. The effect was peculiar – not unpleasant, exactly, but a little as if the place were hiding its feelings. Everywhere were men and women furiously working: hanging garlands, cleaning walls, dusting furniture. Whenever one of them saw Ingrid, he or she would smile and bow and say, "Welcome back, Countess." (What they actually said was "*Isten hozott, Grofné*," which she understood, of course. Ingrid, her grandmother, and Laszlo were the only ones who spoke English. But it suddenly seemed to her the maids and menservants were speaking English, and this reminded her of Gabor, who had spoken English, and who was waiting for her.)

When they reached Ingrid's bedroom, Countess Liliane said, "You should sleep, my dear. You must be exhausted. Why, I slept for two days when I returned from the maze."

"I am tired," Ingrid said, "but I want to speak to my parents."

"You will speak to them shortly," said her grandmother. "I will send for them as soon as I leave you. My dear child, I could not refuse you anything."

"But I need to speak to them now," said Ingrid, "before I go back to the labyrinth."

"Oh," Countess Liliane said, "*that* I could never let you do. The door to the maze is locked. I locked it when you went in, and will not unlock it. And, of course, the other door cannot be opened from the outside."

"But I want to go back," said Ingrid.

Countess Liliane stiffened. Her back was as straight as a lamppost.

"I have told you," she said. "You cannot return. Think what it would do to your parents. Think what it would do to me."

Countess Liliane sighed and all the stiffness went out of her. "Yes, you are your father's daughter," she said. "Your father . . . my son . . . was quite cross when I did not allow him to return. But no mother could send her child to live in a dark maze. I have not always been a good mother, perhaps, but I loved my son enough to spare him that."

"But was my father angry he couldn't go back?"

"Oh, yes. He would not speak to me for months. He looked everywhere for the key. And if I had not hidden it in a very secret place, he would certainly have gone back on his own. And now that I see you are exactly like him, I must hide it from you as well. But I forgive you, my dear. I forgive you."

The countess called for a butler, who approached with

a square of chocolate and a glass of deep yellow liquor on a dark platter.

"This is a royal Tokay," said the countess. "You must drink it down at once."

The wine was like a cool and tart grape juice, but it made Ingrid's head feel light.

"You must sleep, my Ingrid. When you wake, we will celebrate the return of Countess Balazs."

She pulled the covers up to Ingrid's chin and stood up.

"Everything you see belongs to you," she said. "But you must forget about your Gabor. He will get along fine without you."

Her grandmother's words were sensible. Ingrid could imagine her parents' distress if anything were to happen, if she were to return underground.

Would it be so wrong if she did not return? Who would blame her?

And yet, how could it be noble to break a promise? And what did it mean that Gabor allowed himself to hope for her return?

And yet, who knew when it was right to be selfish?

20

Sleep

With all she'd been through, all the excitement and fear, you wouldn't think Ingrid could manage sleep. But sleep she did. Once her grandmother left the room, sleep descended as if it were carried in the flowers beside her bed.

And what a strange sleep it was. . . .

When she closed her eyes, she dreamed she was in the room she was really in. She could see herself on the bed, eyes closed. She could touch the white flowers beside her sleeping self. But when she did, the flowers coughed and said, "*Grofné . . . Grofné . . . ,*" which is to say, "Countess . . . Countess. . . ."

Then Gabor was in the room with her. He said, "You have not forgotten me, have you, Countess?"

But he didn't seem all that concerned. If he hadn't been a wolf, you would have said he was smiling. "I adore being in dreams," he said.

Ingrid was confused.

"Am I in your dream, Gabor, or are you in mine?"

"It makes no difference, Countess. It is wonderful to dream together, don't you think?"

"Yes," said Ingrid.

It really *did* feel wonderful. It felt as if she and Gabor shared a deep secret.

"There is something I must show you, Countess, but we know so little of each other. I do not know your home."

"My home?"

As soon as Ingrid thought of home, a wall in her dream room disappeared, and outside there was water. She and Gabor were on the shore of Lake Ontario.

"It is lovely, Countess, but where is the forest? You must tell me about your home, when you and I are alone together."

Ingrid was confused. "When will we be alone?" she asked.

"When you return to the labyrinth," said Gabor.

This is certainly a dream, thought Ingrid, and, as she remembered she was dreaming, the wall returned. She and Gabor were again in her bedroom, looking down at her sleeping self.

"There is something I must show you," said Gabor. "You must follow me, if you are to keep your word."

She followed Gabor out of her bedroom. It was exactly as if she were awake, but Ingrid knew she was dreaming because, from time to time, one of the flowers along the wall would cough and politely ask if she needed anything, anything at all, until Gabor growled and said, "Quiet, you lilies. Can't you see the countess must pay attention?"

When they reached a back door to the mansion, they stepped outside. The world was warm and sunlit. There was a single, fluffy cloud in the sky. It was shaped like a kitten, then a saucer, then a wedding dress, and finally, a pair of shoes.

"This way, Countess," said Gabor. He led her away from the mansion to a stone house.

In the small stone house, there was a room full of linen, a room full of tables and chairs, and three empty rooms upstairs. They went to the room filled with linen. Gabor nudged a closet door with his muzzle, and Ingrid opened it.

The closet was large, almost a room in itself, but its four walls were covered with long hooks and on each and every hook there were four or five keys. The keys were of every imaginable type: gold, silver, brass, iron. There were keys so tiny, they fit into Ingrid's palm, like a ladybug. There were keys so big, they went from Ingrid's elbow to the tip of her longest finger.

She had never seen so many keys. The walls, covered by keys, looked like the sides of very strange fish.

"Is this real?" she asked.

"Yes, it is," said Gabor. "When you wake up, Countess, you must come to this room on your own. The key to the labyrinth is this one."

Gabor lifted his paw and pointed to an unremarkable gold key that was the fifth key on the fifth hook from the ground on the seventh hook from the corner on the wall facing the closet door.

Gabor said, "Fifth key. Fifth hook. Seventh hook from the corner. Every day, Countess Liliane changes the place of this one key. But today, you will find it here. I hope Countess Ingrid will not forget her promise to me."

Gabor bowed down before her.

"Will you hurt me?" asked Ingrid.

"I am a wolf," said Gabor. "I do as wolves do."

"What do wolves do?" asked Ingrid.

"They are faithful," said Gabor. "And fierce. They are tame to those who are true."

As he spoke these words, Ingrid's dream faded, leaving only darkness and sleep.

In this dream, Gabor had been kind and considerate. He had spoken to her as a friend would, but what would the real Gabor do if she returned to the maze?

That was a different question – a question she thought of as her dream faded and deeper sleep came on.

21

Two Keys

When Ingrid woke, it seemed to her she had been sleeping for days. She'd been asleep for only five hours, but she was no longer tired, and she remembered every moment of her dream with Gabor. The dream was so vivid, she half-expected the flowers in her room to cough.

Almost as soon as Ingrid opened her eyes, her grandmother entered. The Countess Liliane wore a long yellow dress with a stiff, blue lace collar, blue lace cuffs, and a blue lace hem.

Seeing Ingrid awake, she smiled and asked, "Did you sleep well?"

"Oh, yes," said Ingrid. "Very well."

"How wonderful, my dear. And did you dream?"

"I don't remember," said Ingrid.

"Oh, I am certain you remember every detail," said the countess. "Your Gabor showed you exactly where to find the key to the labyrinth, did he not? You know, child, every Balazs has the same dream. The wolf tells everyone where to find the key."

She sat beside Ingrid and held her granddaughter's hand. "He seemed kind, didn't he? I remember how lovely it was to dream of the wolf. It was sad to abandon him in the labyrinth, but I believe my parents did the right thing. If they hadn't stopped me, your father would not exist . . . and neither would you. If you were to go, think how tragic for your own children, who will never be born. You would not be my granddaughter, if you did not wish to return, but I would not be your grandmother if I allowed you to go back. And so, my dear, I have moved the key. It is no longer in the linen room, where it was."

Ingrid was suddenly and inexpressibly sad. She did not want to cry, exactly, but her grandmother, who perhaps at one time had felt as she was feeling now, drew her close and Ingrid cried, her tears dampening the front of her grandmother's yellow dress.

"It will pass. It will pass," said Countess Liliane.

To Ingrid it didn't seem that her sadness would ever pass. She wished her father were here to comfort her, to tell her what he had done. She missed him most, now that she understood something of what his childhood had been, and she wondered again why he had left his home and if her sadness really would pass.

"You're still sad," said Ingrid.

"Yes, my dear, I am sad, but I am sad for my own reasons."

"Why?"

"Because I miss my son."

"Were you angry when he married my mother?"

"Oh, no, not at all. Did he say so?"

"Yes," said Ingrid.

"That was not it at all," said Countess Liliane. "I was angry because he married without so much as asking me. It is true I would have preferred he marry someone of his own station, but he and Krysztina ran off without so much as a word to me, his own mother. I was most offended. When you were born, he sent me a postcard, and that offended me again. Is it right that a man should send his mother a postcard at the birth of her grandchild?"

This did not sound like her father, nor like her mother. They had both taught her to be considerate of others.

Countess Liliane pouted, exactly as if she were a child whose plaything had been taken from her. But then she said, "We do not need to speak of such things now. You have come back from the labyrinth. We must celebrate."

As if she had just thought of it, Ingrid asked, "Has anyone ever been . . . eaten by the wolf?"

"Oh, yes," said her grandmother. "Any who wish it may enter the labyrinth, but only the Balazses return."

"Why would anyone else go?"

"Because we must share our fortune with any who return. It is the custom."

"But how do you know they were eaten by the wolf?"

"My dear, there are no other beasts in the maze."

"What about the crows?"

"The crows? I dare say there are crows, and they *are* outsized, but they will not eat you. Listen, child, you must give up the idea of a return. I will not allow it. I have hidden the key. It is best if we celebrate the young countess' return. I have kept my own dress from the time I was your age. The girls will bring it in a moment."

Countess Liliane kissed Ingrid's hand.

"I have sent for your parents, child. Though I despise the telephone, I have had Laszlo use one of the telephones in Liliana. He has assured me your parents will be here as soon as they are able to escape from work."

Ingrid allowed her grandmother to kiss her cheek. She was gratified her father and grandmother were drawing close. She might have been happy, even, were it not for Gabor and her promise and the words Gabor had spoken. She was different. What could that mean?

"Now," said the countess, "let us begin."

She clapped her hands and three young girls came into the room. One carried a dress almost identical to the one Countess Liliane wore, save that this dress was blue and the collar, cuffs, and hem yellow. The second carried a necklace of black pearls and a dark tiara. The third brought a pair of elegant blue shoes, shoes that fit perfectly.

It would have been so simple to forget Gabor. Her grandmother seemed a changed woman, kinder to her but also less harsh with the men and women who ran about seeing to every little detail: flowers, water, perfume, drawing the curtains, raising the windows so a breeze that smelled of lavender could go through the mansion.

It would have been simple to lose herself in happiness. Her parents were coming. Soon she would see them in the place they had come from. How wonderful to walk the hills and towns with her mother and father. They would show her where they had met and . . .

The thought of Gabor was insistent. Ingrid felt as if she were betraying a friend, with each moment she was away from the maze. She had promised to return and she could not, in her heart, believe Gabor would hurt her, and she could not stand the thought of him alone in his labyrinth.

There had to be a way to find the key. But where could her grandmother have hidden it?

As Ingrid walked downstairs with her grandmother, she heard the voices of what seemed to be hundreds of people talking at once. And, in fact, the mansion was filled with people.

Everyone was formally dressed. The women wore black gowns. The men wore tuxedos. And all of them had, pinned to their lapels or dresses, carnations or red lilies.

And another thing: they were all rather . . . old.

No, they were ancient. Ingrid's grandmother was one of the youngest people in the room.

As she was introduced to Monsieur le Marquis du Vieux Panache and Madame la Comtesse de la Tour du Moulin, Ingrid began to feel a little overwhelmed. There were so many people, it would take hours to shake each and every hand.

Her elders looked down on her kindly and cradled her hand in theirs, pleased to meet the young countess at last. One woman began to cry, when introduced to Ingrid, not because of anything Ingrid did but because Ingrid so resembled the young Liliane, the woman was reminded of her own (lost) childhood.

The counts and countesses, dukes and duchesses, marquises and marquesses were all very friendly, but well beyond the years when they could, comfortably, entertain a child. So, though it was her evening, and though the reception and dinner were in her honor, Ingrid soon found herself a little bored.

Who would have thought, after the day she'd had, she could be bored? And yet, if her grandmother hadn't kept her close and brought her into most every conversation, Ingrid might have fallen asleep on one of the three – no, *four* – yellow sofas in the large room.

As far as Ingrid could tell, everyone was talking about "the old days," about the times when they had all been happiest. She had no idea what those times were like, so when a man said, "Oh, you dear girl, how happy you would have been. What days we had," all she could do was smile politely until he turned away.

Then, just as she was wondering whether or not she could go to her room without being noticed, Ingrid looked down at her feet. There, on the polished wooden floor, was a small kitten that seemed to have wandered in among the guests. It was adorable: a handful of black fur, with one snowy paw, as if it had stepped in a cloud.

She bent down to pick the kitten up, but it moved out of her reach. It skittered away from her, rubbing itself against hems, shoes, and crutches as it went. No one seemed to notice it, save Ingrid. Or maybe they did notice, but the others ignored the little creature as it rubbed and mewed its way across the room.

Excusing herself as she went, Ingrid followed the kitten out of the room and away from the gathering. She had not held a kitten in so long, she ached to touch its soft fur and feel the beating of its heart.

Ingrid followed the kitten along a bright florid hall, down two cloud-white steps, and into a room she didn't know. The kitten was playing. From time to time, it jumped up and down as if it were trying to catch a mouse or were being attacked by an invisible foe. But when it came to the room, the kitten went straight to an open clothes closet where, beneath the clothes, was a small saucer of milk.

Ingrid followed the kitten to the closet.

"Oh, you must be hungry," she said. And she ran her fingers along its arched back.

The kitten looked up from the saucer, rubbed its neck against Ingrid's knee, purred, and went back to its milk.

Ingrid watched as the kitten drank, but . . .

As she waited, she had the strange feeling she'd been here, in this very room, before. There was something familiar. The kitten, the saucer, and . . . as she looked up, she saw a beautiful wedding dress and beneath the dress: a pair of elegant white shoes.

Without thinking, Ingrid put her hand inside the left shoe and took out, as if it had been left for her, the key to the labyrinth. And no sooner did she touch the key than everything came back to her: her dream, Gabor, the cloud that had been kitten, saucer, dress, and shoe, and the key itself – the one she had dreamed and the one she now held in her hand.

It was a remarkable feeling, holding the real key. It was like seeing something shining underwater and pulling it up to have a look. The key was more dull, in real life, but it was a little unreal, too.

How did Ingrid know *this* was the key to the labyrinth?

She knew, the same way one knows a particular piece will fit into a puzzle. She set out for the dungeon at once, to prove it to herself and to keep her word to Gabor.

22

Gabor Surprised

You might think Ingrid would have a difficult time finding her way back to the labyrinth. After all, she was in a room she didn't know, in a part of the mansion she did not recognize. Yet, once she stepped out of the kitten's room, she turned right instead of left, went down a familiar stairwell, and, as easily as if she'd known the place all her life, found herself in the flower-filled room with two doors: one leading to the labyrinth, the other out of it.

A peculiar moment . . .

Ingrid was about to re-enter the maze to find a wolf who believed she would return. Why?

Had she bid her parents good-bye?

No.

Had she listened to her grandmother's words?

Yes. No one returned to the labyrinth. It was not done. It was wrong to endanger her own life. What if, this time, she did not come out again?

And yet . . . there were things one did that one *hoped* were right. (When she had used glue to fix a cup she had broken: her mother's favorite blue teacup.)

There were things one *guessed* were right. (Had it been right to tell Principal Milton that Dan Jones had pushed Alex McLeish into the mud?)

There were things one *knew* were right.

And, finally, there were things one *felt* were right.

This was a thing Ingrid felt was right. Aside from the excitement she felt at having found the key, she held on to Gabor's final words to her, that she was different, that he hoped she would return. If she was not meant to do so, why had she, of all the Balazses, been the only one to find the key?

She wished she had spoken to her father before going back, but she was certain he would have done as she was doing, if he had been the one to find the key.

The labyrinth was still bewildering. The torch was exactly where it had been and she took it down, but Ingrid left the door open as she wandered along the corridor.

The light and the scent of flowers accompanied her until the first curve. Then, the maze took over and the darkness deepened. Ingrid walked slowly, afraid the torch would go out and, as she walked, she called, "Gabor . . . Gabor. . . ."

She had no idea where she would find him, no idea what she would say when she did.

"Gabor," she said, opening the door to the first room. And "Gabor," she said, as she opened the door to the second.

And there he was, in the middle of the room with its four candles. When he heard his name, Gabor looked up as if to ask, *What*?

In his mouth was the severed wing of the crow he was, at that moment, eating. Like a child caught with a handful of cookies, Gabor dropped the wing. He growled and pounced at her.

Ingrid had no time to speak before Gabor was upon her. He pushed her against a wall and bit her shoulder.

"Please . . . ," was all Ingrid managed, before she began to cry – cry because she had been bitten and cry because her first thought was that she would never see her parents again.

Gabor took his teeth from her shoulder and stepped

back. "Countess," he said, "is it really you? What are you doing here?"

Ingrid could not answer, as she could not stop crying. It would have been odd if she *had* managed to stop crying, but it was especially difficult because she was in pain, because she was thinking of her home and her parents, and because blood had stained the front of her grandmother's dress.

Gabor was suddenly uncertain.

"Has the countess returned in order to be eaten?"

"No. I didn't come to be eaten," cried Ingrid. "I came because I promised to come back."

"But no one has ever come back," said Gabor. "You truly do *not* wish to be eaten?"

"Yes," said Ingrid.

He stepped towards her and then, near enough to bite, he walked around her and back to where he'd been. In other words, the wolf paced . . . from Ingrid to the mass of crow feathers.

Ingrid kept quiet and still until, after a few minutes, Gabor stopped before her and said, "I am confused, Countess. You have come because you gave your word. You are truly noble, but what is there for you here but darkness and confusion? I cannot think you wish to live on bread and mice. Yet, none of your kind has kept his word with me. They have all sent their children here, so the Balazses would prosper. They have always remembered their history with the wolves, yes. But you, Countess, have treated me with respect, without considering how difficult it would be for you to stay with me. There are no words to describe my dismay, and my gratitude."

Gabor bowed as deeply as he could.

"The labyrinth is the only home I have had for centuries," he said, "but I will leave it. I was left here to make certain the Balazses continue to speak to wolves. My brethren were so charmed by Countess Nadja, so convinced of her nobility, they spared her and her family, and brought them great fortune . . . all because Countess Nadja deigned to speak with us as equals. In two hundred and ninety years, none of the Balazses has been as noble as Countess Nadja. None, before you."

Again, Gabor bowed deeply.

"I am honored the Countess Ingrid has returned," he said. "From this moment, I shall be her faithful servant."

Ingrid did not know what to do. Her fright turned to relief and then perplexity. What did it mean that he would leave the labyrinth to be her servant?

How would he serve her?

Would he follow her about?

What would her friends say? Perhaps her father could convince Gabor to stay here, in the Old World.

In the meantime, what should she do?

Ingrid was so stunned by the turn of events, she followed Gabor out of the maze without an "if" or an "and" or a "but."

23

A Countess Surprised

"But," said Ingrid, "how can you leave your home?"

She and Gabor had closed the door to the labyrinth behind them and, now, it seemed to Ingrid she'd been wrong to return, wrong to bring Gabor from his home, wrong to listen only to what was inside of her.

Though she had done everything she'd felt was right, it now felt as if she had betrayed her grandmother and Gabor and perhaps even her parents.

Was it possible to be both wrong *and* right?

"I do regret leaving," said Gabor, thoughtfully. "But I must. For some time, I have served the Balazs family.

Now, I will serve its greatest member, the only one who has returned. It is true that, in the labyrinth, I did not grow old and, now that I am outside, I shall begin to die, but at least, Countess, I shall die in the company of one I admire. Besides, I truly was tired of eating mice and crows. The countess is almost certain to feed me other things, is she not?"

"Yes," said Ingrid.

But that was something she had not even begun to think about. What would happen if there was not enough food for Gabor? Would he eat the cats, dogs, and raccoons at home? Or . . .

"Gabor? You won't eat people, will you?"

"The countess is being playful," said Gabor. "People are not delicious."

The voices of the guests grew louder as they ascended the stairs. They had come to the top. It sounded as if Ingrid had not been missed, and she was relieved her grandmother appeared not to have noticed her absence. She went straight to the room where the guests were happily reminiscing and quietly laughing. Gabor followed behind her.

Now, Gabor was not a small wolf. He was large and, what's more, he was somewhat irritable as his eyes were not used to so much light. He could not keep himself from growling as he walked among the guests. So it was not long before everyone in the room knew there was a wild animal amongst them, and this caused real panic.

The first guest to notice Gabor was a gray-haired gentleman, the marquis of Remington, who leaned on a black mahogany cane as he stood talking. When he saw the wolf (and heard its growl), he was stunned. He began to walk backwards from the room and then, when he was far enough away, he turned and ran – quite quickly, for an older gentleman.

"Wolf!" he shouted.

The Baroness von Rund und Zaft was the next to see the wolf. Gabor blinked at her and growled even louder than he had at the marquis. The baroness, rather than run, screamed at the top of her voice and fainted dead away, falling into a thin gentleman who was crushed beneath her. He only had time to say, "Oh, my Lord," before he was smothered.

For a brief, brief moment, there was complete silence. Then, mayhem. All the other guests seemed to see the wolf at once, and those who couldn't actually see Gabor felt his presence. One can usually tell when there is a wild animal in the room. You don't need to see it, and neither did Countess Liliane's guests. They all panicked at once and, out of the mayhem, there came pandemonium.

There were a number of faintings.

Three brothers, each in his eighties, passed out when they heard the wolf's growl.

A duke who thought Ingrid was in danger courageously stood between the wolf and the girl, flicked his lighter, and tried to ward the wolf off with its small flame. "Shoo, wolf!" he said. "Shoo!"

Annoyed, Gabor jumped up on the man and bit his left ear, drawing a pearl of blood.

"Oh, dear, oh, dear," said the duke. And he, too, fainted.

A woman who happened to see the drop of blood jumped up and down, as if Gabor were a mouse. Another woman, who did not see the blood, jumped up and down a few times before, the blood having rushed from her head, she lay down on a long chesterfield and fell asleep.

In the midst of this pandemonium, all those who could ran from the room and, indeed, from the mansion, taking nothing with them but the clothes on their backs – leaving shawls, umbrellas, dinner jackets, and, even, a pair of pants that had been pulled off the Duke de Velha Infancia by a fainting woman who clutched at him as she fell.

In some ten minutes, the reception room, which had been filled with guests, was an untidy place where, here and there, were the nicely clothed bodies of those who had fainted. There were also two Balazses and a wolf.

After a while, Countess Liliane spoke. "What have you done, child? Are you hurt?"

She touched Ingrid's shoulder and Ingrid winced.

"A little," she said. "I went back to the labyrinth."

"I can see that. You have brought the wolf back. You have set him free. It is the end of our family."

"What do you mean, Grandmother?"

"I mean, child, that never again will a Balazs descend to face the wolf. You have put an end to the thing that has made us who we are. So you have put an end to the Balazses."

Countess Liliane sighed as she spoke. Ingrid had taken the wolf from his home and, now, it seemed she had ruined her own family.

Gabor said, "Excuse me, Countess, but that is not so. The Balazses will go on. It will be different, but it is always different. You are not your son, Count Sandor. And the count is not his daughter, Countess Ingrid. It is surprising that a Balazs has set me free, but so it is. As for me, I am grateful. In the few minutes I have been here, I see how much I have missed. I will be forever loyal to the young countess who has liberated me."

Gabor bowed. "But why," he asked, "were your guests so impolite? Have they never seen a wolf?"

To anyone looking on, the sight would have been unusual: an old woman and a young girl stood in the center of a large room talking to a wolf that growled ferociously as they spoke.

More peculiar still: Countess Liliane spoke Hungarian, Ingrid spoke English, and the wolf, understood by both, spoke neither language.

Ingrid was the first to notice. "Gabor," she asked, "are you speaking English?"

"He is speaking Hungarian," said Countess Liliane.

"The countess is wrong," said Gabor. "I do not speak any language. I simply *am*. Some understand me and others do not."

"What about your name, then?" asked Ingrid. "Are you really Gabor or Istvan?"

"The young countess is clever," said Gabor, "but I have no name, either. Different people have given me different names. But the young countess surely knows all this."

"Istvan," said Countess Liliane, "I don't know where I am to keep you. The servants will be most upset."

In fact, at the sight of the wolf, most of the servants had fled. It would be hours before any of them returned and days before they became accustomed to a wolf in the mansion – a wolf that growled unpleasantly at the sight of them and bared his fangs whenever they drew close to Ingrid.

Politely, Gabor said, "I am sorry, but the countess is misinformed. I will remain only if Countess Ingrid remains. I will leave if she leaves. I will have no other mistress."

Of the servants who remained, only Laszlo was unafraid of the wolf.

On first meeting Gabor, Laszlo bowed and said, when Ingrid hit him, "Will the Countess Ingrid please inform His Excellency the wolf that I am honored to meet him?"

When Ingrid told Gabor, Gabor answered, "And I am surprised to meet such an ancient man. He smells quite sour."

Ingrid did not translate. Instead, she watched as Gabor and Laszlo bowed to each other, both trying to be polite, though neither spoke the other's language.

24

A Son Returns

It was a peculiar thing, this constant wolf.

For days, Ingrid jumped whenever Gabor growled, or tripped over him when she forgot he was there. It was a perplexing and a distracting thing.

Gabor allowed her to bathe on her own, mostly because she insisted. He thought her modesty unnecessary and inexplicable. He lay down outside the white sheets, keeping guard as she bathed.

If any of the servants showed the slightest disrespect to Ingrid, Gabor would pounce on them. One poor man served Ingrid's peas on the right-hand side rather than the left. Gabor knocked him down and sent the peas flying. A chambermaid entered Ingrid's room without knocking. Gabor bounded towards her, snarling, his fangs bared. The poor woman saw her life pass before her eyes and fainted dead away.

In the days that followed Gabor's release from the labyrinth, the chambermaids, butlers, cooks, stable-hands, and gardeners were the ones that suffered most. They did not understand Gabor, could not speak his language, and so unwillingly found themselves in the presence of a touchy and terrifying animal. Gabor ruined their workplace, and some resigned rather than face the prospect of running into the wolf in a dark corridor or dimly lit room.

For Ingrid, it was as though she herself had changed. Everyone began to approach her with care. It was painful to see how many were afraid of her, of her company.

She spoke to Gabor. She forbade him to jump up on the butlers and chambermaids but, really, though he was wise, Gabor was a wolf. He knew death, but not custom, nor politesse, nor patience. When he thought Ingrid needed protection, he was ferocious in her defense.

On the other hand, the bond between them was remarkable. Though Gabor was her protector and so much older, he was, in some ways, like a younger brother to Ingrid. He had lived most of his life in the labyrinth. He knew very little about the world. So, he was, for instance, delighted to discover the flowers and trees around the mansion. He could barely keep himself from rolling in the purple-headed lavender that grew by a side entrance. When there was no one around but the two of them, he ran about wildly, playing in the tall grasses.

"I have not done this since I was a cub," he said. "It is wonderful."

He listened closely when Ingrid explained why some women wore dresses and men pants, and he was amazed by her knowledge of the world. (Of course, he was, later, offended when he saw a man in a kilt and would have torn the kilt from him had Ingrid not told him it would be wrong to do so.)

And he was fascinated by stories of Canada, with its polar bears and horseflies and ice houses in which men caught slow cold fish.

"I will go with the countess to Canada," he said, "for as long as the countess desires. But the countess must promise one thing. I respectfully ask only this."

"What is it?" asked Ingrid.

"Now that I am no longer in the labyrinth, I will die. But the countess must understand that I must not die anywhere but here. You must bury me among the lime trees at the bottom of the hill. Do you see them?"

"Yes, Gabor, but it'll be a long time before you die, won't it?"

"Ah," said Gabor, "this I do not know, but I trust you will bring me here to die. Otherwise, my soul will not find peace."

Though Ingrid did not really understand what Gabor was asking, though she was too young to understand why a soul needs peace, she said, "Yes, Gabor. I'll bring you back."

And they went on talking about Ingrid's home: Toronto, fish on the shore of a lake, houses built so close together you could – as her father said – spit in your neighbor's window, snowmen, iceboats, iceberg lettuce. . . .

"Save for the spitting, it sounds marvelous," said Gabor.

And, after a while, it was as if Ingrid had known the wolf for a long time.

Gabor spent most of his time with Ingrid, but he was, when not angry, a gregarious wolf.

For instance, he spoke to Liliane as one would to an acquaintance, listened to her thoughts about the world, and learned, at last, that many of the Balazses who'd passed through the labyrinth had been prevented from returning by their parents.

This was not, strictly speaking, true. Very few of the Balazses had ever sought to return. Most had been too frightened or, as Countess Liliane had been, too respectful of their parents' wishes to attempt a return. However, even those who had not returned sometimes wished they had had the courage to do so.

"But you," said Gabor, "I remember you as haughty. You would not speak to me. I do not believe you ever wished to return."

"Yes," said Countess Liliane, "there was so much I did not know when I was a child. I thought that you, Gabor, were a servant. And I was wrong. Can you forgive me?"

"I would have bitten you," said Gabor, "if I had not forgiven you."

"You wouldn't have eaten me, surely?"

"No, I would have bitten you," said Gabor, "but I certainly would have felt sorry . . . afterwards."

"Ah," said Countess Liliane, "here is Ingrid with your supper."

Her parents' return was wonderful, but it was strangely familiar as well, as if Ingrid had dreamed the return or had wished for it so passionately it had already settled in her imagination.

A week passed before they could come, a week during which Ingrid and Gabor became acquainted with each other and the grounds and the mansion. It was even more interesting, for Ingrid, to have someone with her to see the silver dresses, the book about water, the little theater.

On the day her parents were to arrive, Ingrid waited for hours, Gabor by her side, watching for the approach of the car and Laszlo and her mother and father.

Her grandmother waited with them until, tired of sitting, she wandered off to see (once more) if the house was properly cleaned and decorated. "You must not come inside," she said to Gabor. "You'll rattle the maids."

As they waited, Ingrid asked Gabor about his life underground.

"Oh," he said, "there is nothing to tell. I was there for centuries. I ate mice and I wandered through the maze."

"Did you ever get lost?"

"No, Countess. It was not possible to lose my way. That is the problem with knowing a place too well. I knew each and every one of the rooms. I could tell which one I was in by smell alone."

"But what did you do all day?"

"Oh, the countess will be disappointed. I am afraid I did very little. I ate and I thought. I thought and I ate."

"What did you think about?"

"I thought about food and the Balazses I had met, and I thought about time – how very like a crow it is."

"Time is like a crow?"

"Why yes, Countess, it is. One moment it stands still. Then, a short time is long. At other moments, it flutters about, jumping here and there. And then time passes without your knowing and you are suddenly hungry."

"I've noticed that," said Ingrid. "When I'm doing something interesting, the time goes so quickly I don't notice it at all."

"Now that I am no longer in the labyrinth," said Gabor, "I am too distracted to think about time as it passes. The young countess has told me so much that is unexpected. I am not certain how I will survive in the ice and snow of your home, but I am grateful for the chance to see what few wolves have seen."

Ingrid was about to tell him that, well, there *were* wolves in Canada, that they looked very like him, that there were quite a number of them, when . . .

"There," said Gabor. "The car is coming. That will be your parents, Countess."

And so it was. The dark car, driven by Laszlo, made its way up the hill.

Ingrid might have run toward the car, but Gabor did not yet trust automobiles. As soon as she got up, he snapped at her dress, holding her back as a parent might hold a child who runs toward traffic.

The car came to a stop and, slowly, two of its doors opened.

Ingrid's father was the first to emerge. He blinked in the sunlight and then offered his arm to his wife, who emerged from the car as if from darkness.

Every detail of this moment would remain with Ingrid forever: the sun so bright it made the leaves on the trees seem translucent; a warm wind that smelled of lavender and cut grass; the sound of a single bird calling from its perch in a cherry tree. . . .

Then, her parents smiled and came towards her, her mother's arms wide-open, her father looking on, embarrassed as he always was when his emotions got the better of him.

None of them could think what to say . . . or, rather, there were so many things to say, no one could decide what to say first. Instead, Krysztina began to cry and, seeing her mother's tears, Ingrid too might have cried except that, out of the corner of her eye, she could see her father staring at Gabor.

"Gregor?" said her father.

"Yes," answered the wolf. "Welcome home, Count Sandor."

25

A Short Stay in Balazs Mansion

It seemed to Ingrid that her grandmother had, in a short time, become a generous woman. The Countess Liliane was capable of great kindness (to Ingrid) because she saw herself in her granddaughter. In being kind to Ingrid, she was being kind to a Balazs – a member of her own family.

It wasn't as if the countess' haughtiness and pride vanished. Rather, they went a little way underground. Her pride and haughtiness returned, however, as soon as she saw her son (whom she could forgive) and his wife (whom she would not).

When she greeted her daughter-in-law, she extended a cold hand and said (coldly), "A pleasure."

But, then, Krysztina was, to Countess Liliane, an unworthy girl – one who had, somehow, stolen her son's heart. For Ingrid's sake she was civil, but she could not put aside her dislike.

Ingrid's mother, however, was more frightened of the wolf than she was of the countess. She could not speak to Gabor, as the others did. She stood by as her husband and daughter growled at the animal and listened to its low growlings. It was all so strange, it seemed to Krysztina the wolf might, at any moment, pounce at one of them.

Whenever she was near the animal, she stood still and, when it looked at her, she felt dread.

Gabor could no more understand Krysztina than she could understand him. As Ingrid's mother, she was, in a sense, precious to the wolf. He would have done most anything she asked. At one point, he approached and bowed before her.

"What's it doing? What's it doing?" Krysztina cried.

"He's bowing to you," said Ingrid.

"Wonderful," Krysztina said. But she didn't think it wonderful at all.

Immediately upon their arrival, Sandor and Krysztina were shown to their room.

Krysztina was not at all comfortable. The mansion made her feel like a peasant, someone who didn't deserve the attention lavished on her, and she could barely wash her face without a servant rushing in to help her dry it off. She remembered the way her own parents had looked up to the Balazses, wishing nothing more for their daughter than a good position at the mansion.

Now, here she was, a member of the family.

Sandor, on the other hand, was fascinated by Gabor. From the first words the wolf had spoken, Sandor was transfixed. Here was a living part of his childhood. It was as if his land were speaking to him, as it had when he was eleven. Only now, the wolf was outside the labyrinth, freed by Ingrid, Ingrid who had been more brave, more resourceful than he had been at her age.

For most of that first evening, Count Sandor did nothing but speak to his mother, his daughter, and the wolf. He had a thousand questions to ask: How had Ingrid found the key to the labyrinth? Why hadn't she and the wolf remained underground? And how was the countess, his mother, getting along?

All of his questions were interesting, but they were frustrating to Ingrid, who had a thousand questions of her own. She asked the first one, as soon as it was polite: "How are we going to take Gabor home with us?"

Her father said, "We can't take . . . Gabor to Canada."

"No," said Krysztina, "I really don't think we can."

"But we have to," said Ingrid.

It was then that the wolf growled and said, "It is not my place to insist, Count Sandor, but I must go with Countess Ingrid as her servant and protector."

"Ah," said Count Sandor, "you must do as Ingrid says, if you are her servant."

"True," said the wolf, "but I will not leave her."

"I don't see how we are to smuggle a wolf into the country," said the count. "We would have to disguise you, and I cannot think of a convincing disguise for a wolf."

"Why must you go at all?" said Countess Liliane. "Stay here, all of you. *This* is your home."

"It *was* our home, Mother. We must return to Canada. Our lives are there."

Countess Liliane glared (briefly) at her daughter-in-law, as if it were Krysztina's fault they had moved away, Krysztina's fault it had taken so long for her, Countess Liliane Montesquieu von Puffdorf di Turbino de la Louve des Balazs, to see her granddaughter.

"Of course," said the countess. "You must return to Canada, but after that you must return home."

"We'll see," said her son.

"We shall see, indeed," said Countess Liliane. "But let us speak of other things. I would like to make your daughter my heir. When she comes of age, Countess Ingrid Montesquieu von Puffdorf di Turbino de la Louve des Balazs will inherit everything I own."

"But you'll still be alive then, won't you?" asked Ingrid.

"I do not hope so," said Countess Liliane, "but if I still live, the young countess will have to share with the old. Is that acceptable?"

Ingrid blushed. "Oh, yes," she said.

Countess Liliane took her granddaughter's hand and kissed it. "Do you understand what this means, child?"

"Yes, I think so," said Ingrid. "But, maybe, not really. . . ."

"It means," said her father, "that, in a few years, everything here will belong to you."

"Everything here and all that I have saved," said Countess Liliane. "And I have saved a considerable amount. You will be one of the wealthiest women in Europe, my dear child. But there are conditions to your inheritance."

"What conditions can there be?" asked Sandor.

"Countess Ingrid has passed the trials of her nobility. She has shown proper couth at table, she has found *A History of the Balazses*, and she has returned from the labyrinth. But Countess Ingrid has also freed the wolf. No one else has done this. And so, Ingrid must now be responsible for Gabor. She will receive no help from me. Wherever she chooses to live, she and she alone will care for the wolf. When Countess Ingrid comes of age, she will inherit everything, but only if she returns to Liliana. If she does not return, Ingrid Balazs will inherit nothing. I will leave everything to her children."

"But, by all rights, *I* should inherit," said Sandor.

"You have forsaken your home and title," said Countess Liliane. "Not so?"

"Yes," said Sandor, "however . . ."

His mother did not smile.

"You have no say in my decision," she said. "I leave all to Ingrid, but on condition. Do you understand, Ingrid?"

Ingrid, who did not know what to make of all this, nodded her head as sagely as she could.

"Good . . . very good," said Countess Liliane. "Now, let us have tea."

She took up a small silver bell and shook it. It made a small piercing sound and, after a while, a slightly nervous butler looked in to inquire after their needs.

"Madam called?" he said.

But he kept his eye on the wolf.

Ingrid's family was reunited. They were going home together. There was still the matter of Gabor (how *do* you travel with a wolf?) and the fact she would soon be leaving her grandmother, but Ingrid should have been pleased.

Yet, she was not quite happy.

No, that's not right. Ingrid was *happy* when she thought of certain things (her parents, Gabor's company, the affection her grandmother had for her . . .). She was *confused* when she thought of others (the fear Gabor aroused in the butlers and maids, the idea of her inheritance . . .). And she was *saddened* by the discomfort her mother felt in the Balazs mansion.

Two days after her parents' arrival, she asked, "Gabor, why doesn't grandmother like my mother?"

The wolf, who was just then licking the dirt from his paws, considered the question. "The Countess Liliane is a proud woman," he said. "She would not say so, but I believe she is unhappy to be left on her own . . . without her son, or her granddaughter, or even myself, who lived so far beneath her. Perhaps she believes our leaving is your mother's fault, and this has caused resentment."

"Why doesn't Grandmother come with us?"

"It is not easy to leave home, Countess, especially when one is old."

This did explain her grandmother's behavior, but Ingrid was still concerned for her mother, her mother who seemed happiest talking to the maids and to Laszlo, her mother who seemed to find it difficult to speak to her own husband, in this place where he was "Count Sandor."

Would her mother find it difficult to speak with *her*, now that she was Countess Ingrid, her grandmother's heir?

When they had been together for three days, and when Count Sandor had made peace with his mother, Ingrid suggested they visit *her* mother's home, the place Krysztina had been raised.

Krysztina, embarrassed, said, "It doesn't exist anymore, sweetheart."

Countess Liliane added, "Yes, that is quite correct. It was torn down after your mother's parents died."

But Sandor said, "We should go, anyway. It would be good for Ingrid to see her mother's home or, at least, the place where it used to be."

They set out the next morning, walking from the mansion: down the hill and through a cool and dark little wood. Gabor walked beside Ingrid, of course, and both of them were behind the adults. Krysztina walked a little ways in front, leading them, and behind her were her husband and his mother.

The day was bright and the blue sky was visible just above the treetops. When they emerged from the wood, the land was flat and green and they walked along a narrow gravel road past old farmhouses and fields until they came to a sign that said PETÖFI.

Krysztina stopped and said, "This is the village where I grew up."

"Where?" asked Ingrid.

"All around," her mother answered.

As far as Ingrid could see, there was nothing: no stores, no houses, no buildings.

"Yes," said Countess Liliane, as if she was remembering something far in the past. "This is where Petöfi used to be."

"What happened to the town?" asked Ingrid.

"Well, it's been some time, but . . . the town was bought by Roberto de la Corte. You remember him, Sandor? The little man with the mustache. He was going to turn Petöfi into a lovely resort, but he died after all the buildings were demolished, and now . . . there is nothing."

The sun was so bright the path ahead of them looked pale. Krysztina led them along what was left of the roads. Every once in a while, she and Sandor would recognize a piece of wall or the remains of a garden, but, really, the little village was no more and, try as she might, Ingrid could not imagine what it had looked like.

When they had wandered amongst the weeds and debris for some time, Ingrid's mother stopped before a pile of stones and wood.

"This was my home," she said.

How different from the home Ingrid might inherit. And how sad. Ingrid took her mother's hand and they stood together beside the ruins.

"How did you and Dad meet?" asked Ingrid.

(Strange that they had never told her.)

"We met in church," said Sandor. "I was eleven. It was just before I went to the labyrinth, now that I think of it."

"Is this true?" asked Countess Liliane.

"Of course it is, Mother. Why else was I so happy in church?"

"Why didn't you tell me?"

"If I'd told you, Mother, you would have stopped me going."

"Our families weren't at all alike," said Krysztina. "My parents didn't like me talking to your father. They were embarrassed because he was Count Sandor and I was only a poor girl from Petöfi."

Krysztina and her husband held hands at the memory. How much strife they had borne, how much disapproval, until, in love with Krysztina and frightened his family would pull them apart, Sandor renounced his inheritance, his title, his country. He gave up everything for his wife. And yet, as he thought about it, he was surprised at how easy it had been.

To Ingrid, he said, "We left home much later, of course. And I was sorry to deprive you of your inheritance, but I didn't believe my mother would approve of my marriage and I was too much in love to leave your mother."

"But why did you not simply tell me?" asked Countess Liliane indignantly. "I would not have approved, but I would not have chosen to lose my only son. You went off with this girl. What was I to think? I thought she had turned you against your own family. And you never wrote me, not a word."

"I wrote every week for two years," said Sandor, "even though you never bothered to answer."

Countess Liliane was suddenly silent, before turning red. "It's true," she said. "You did write, but I had Laszlo destroy your letters. I could not stand to read them. I thought you had renounced your own mother."

"I renounced no one," said Sandor. "I gave up this life for a life with Krysztina."

Countess Liliane sighed. All the Balazses were stubborn and willful. How could she scold him for being himself?

The countess smiled and said, "We have both been stubborn, Sandor. But perhaps we can put some of this behind us now."

She took Krysztina's arm in hers, and said, "It is sad what has become of Petöfi, isn't it?"

Now, this was a moment Ingrid delighted in. Her father, mother, grandmother, and, of course, herself, all together. Still . . . there was the question of Gabor.

What *was* one to do with a wolf?

26

The Way Home

In the days that followed, things changed.

Countess Liliane was imperious, but she was aware of it and, as much as she was able, she softened her tone. She would, typically, begin a sentence in the old way, as if she were queen, but then end it humbly. This was a little confusing for the maids and butlers who remained with her. They did not know which to believe – the countess who started the sentence or the one who ended it.

Krysztina began to feel that she did, perhaps, in some small way, belong. And, one day, as they were speaking,

Krysztina actually found it in herself to ask Countess Liliane, "May I call you Mother?"

Countess Liliane turned to her and said, "No. Only my son may call me that, but perhaps 'Countess' is too formal. You may call me Liliane."

This affection was a relief to both Ingrid and her father.

Once he was convinced of their mutual respect, Count Sandor spent his time talking to his mother (bringing up old grievances, but only so as to bury them deeper), or walking about the countryside with Krysztina and Ingrid, or sitting up late to talk about the past with Laszlo.

In the evening, Ingrid would find her father in a plush burgundy chair near a cold fireplace. Beside him, Laszlo sat in a simple wooden chair, smoking a pipe whose stem must have been a foot long. You could feel the affection between them. When the count was called upon to strike Laszlo's back, he did so with little fuss. You might have thought it a handshake, a handshake that made Laszlo wince, it's true, but he winced discreetly, so as not to alarm the count.

There was, in short, a harmony to the mansion.

One evening, just before Ingrid and her parents were to return home, Countess Liliane said, "I have been thinking. It is right that Countess Ingrid, who freed the wolf, should take care of him. But she may require some assistance. If you like, Ingrid, I will send Laszlo to you, if Laszlo is willing, so that he may help you through the first few months with Gabor. Is that acceptable?"

It was not acceptable to Gabor. The wolf thought Laszlo an admirable servant and even allowed the old man to feed him. But Gabor did not think himself a burden and was not pleased to be told Laszlo would "help" to care for him.

Nor was it acceptable to Ingrid. Ingrid did not want Laszlo to lose his home, and she did not want the countess to be left without Laszlo's company. Above all, she sensed Gabor's dislike of the idea that *anyone* should come between them.

"No," said Ingrid. "Thank you, Grandmother, but I'd like to take care of him myself."

"I beg your pardon?" growled Gabor.

"I mean," said Ingrid, "I want Gabor to take care of me."

Countess Liliane smiled. "Very well," she said. "Gabor is your responsibility and you are his."

If there was a cloud over Ingrid's last days, it was her longing for Canada.

"I miss home," she said to Gabor.

It was afternoon and they were walking along one of the forgotten roads of what had been Petöfi.

"The young countess is homesick," said the wolf. "She must return home, or she must stay until she forgets her home."

"I don't really want to go, but I miss Alice and my room and everything. . . ."

She wondered if Alice had missed her and how her summer was going and what she would tell Alice about her own summer. Would she have to take Gabor to school? She did not know what she would do if he insisted on coming with her.

As she stood beside him, it occurred to Ingrid that Gabor was doing for her what she might not have done for anyone: leave behind all she knew. And this is what her parents had done, for love.

"Gabor," she asked, "have you ever been in love?"

The wolf was quiet for a time, but once Ingrid explained how she meant the word "love," Gabor said, "The young countess is quite unusual. In all my years, I have not met a Balazs who has asked me such a thing. Do you believe it is good to think of these things?"

"I don't know," said Ingrid. "Sometimes I just think about them."

"Ah," said the wolf, "it is your nature. I am comforted to hear so, Countess. It is not my nature to think such things. I have never given a thought to what you call love. It is your nature to ask these questions. I am thankful it is not mine."

So saying, Gabor walked a little distance from Ingrid and marked his territory against two narrow oak trees by the side of the road.

"What do you have in Canada that cannot be replaced?" asked Countess Liliane.

"What an odd question," answered Sandor. "We have books and photographs and friends and neighbors, people who have been kind. It is the world Ingrid knows. It would break her heart to abandon it."

The Countess Liliane sighed and said, "Sandor, you exasperate me. Very well, return to your small apartment."

Only it wasn't quite so simple to go home.

There was, still, the matter of Gabor. He *would* not be separated from Ingrid, and he could be quite terrifying when he was angry. They much preferred *not* to anger him, but no one knew how to transport the wolf until Ingrid said, "Dad? If one of us was blind, wouldn't we get to bring our dog on the plane with us?"

Sandor was puzzled by the question. "Yes, I suppose we would," he answered.

"So couldn't someone pretend to be blind and take Gabor?"

"I do not much appreciate being thought a dog," said Gabor.

"It's only pretend," said Ingrid.

"It is undignified," said Gabor.

Undignified or not, however, Ingrid persuaded him to pretend. Over the wolf's indignant growls, they managed to cut his fur and dye it black so that, at least from a distance, he looked like a dog.

It was Ingrid who pretended to be blind. Once a proper harness was found for the wolf, Ingrid made a point of keeping her eyes closed, so she was truly dependent on Gabor. Of course, things were easier for the two of them than they were for the blind and their dogs. Ingrid could speak to Gabor and, as it was Gabor's only wish to be of service to her, he was scrupulous in keeping Ingrid away from harm.

The only time anyone was hurt during Ingrid's pretense at blindness was when she did not hear Gabor's warning to avoid a spoon that had fallen on the floor. Ingrid stepped on the spoon. It flew up and struck the bridge of her father's nose.

When it came time for Ingrid and Gabor to enter the airport in Budapest and board the plane, no one who didn't know otherwise would have suspected Ingrid was anything but what she pretended to be: a blind young girl with an intimidating dog, a dog that looked very like a wolf . . . when you thought about it. . . .

And so, the question of travel with Gabor was, in the end, resolved.

They seemed to spend days in the airport and then, when it was time for them to board the plane, time began to race.

Laszlo scarcely had time to kiss the young countess' hand.

Ingrid scarcely had time to kiss her grandmother, who was crying.

(What was one to do when adults cried? For some reason, that was the worst. It made Ingrid feel very sad indeed.)

"It is nothing," said Countess Liliane, wiping her eyes with a handkerchief. "It is the air. The air in Budapest is criminal."

She waved them away.

Then, as if by magic, they were on a plane that taxied to the runway and took off, leaving the bright Old World behind them.

27

To Canada

The flight home was, in most every way, different from the flight over.

Ingrid sat in the first row of the plane, where there was room. Gabor lay before her. She would not allow him to move about the cabin and he found this annoying.

He snarled his objections throughout the first part of the trip, but once they reached the ocean, he calmed down and spoke gently to Ingrid, looking for comfort. This was, after all, the first time he had traveled by plane and he found it unnerving.

"What *is* keeping this machinery aloft?" he asked.

"I don't know," said Ingrid. "But we won't fall."

The stewardess was kind, bringing them their dinners and drinks first, helping Ingrid to eat (believing her blind), and feeding hamburger and water to the wolf.

Every so often, Ingrid's father would come up to see how Ingrid and Gabor were getting on. Once, Sandor stayed for some time, to explain aerodynamics to the wolf, but for the most part Ingrid and Gabor were on their own.

Ingrid was restless with anticipation. She described most of the streets she knew and the halls and classrooms of her school. Though she'd been unhappy just months before, she was anxious to return and couldn't wait to tell Alice all that had happened.

You wouldn't have thought it possible for Ingrid to fall asleep and yet . . .

After a few hours, the hum of the engines began to work on her. She was, at first, a little drowsy. She asked Gabor the same question two or three times: *You won't miss home too much, will you, Gabor? You won't miss home will you, Gabor?*

Then she fell into a sound sleep.

Each time Ingrid asked the question, Gabor answered as honestly as he could: "I will certainly miss my home, Countess, but I will be comforted by your friendship. Besides, I have great respect for the country that has given you to the world. I could not but love the place you were born, Countess, and I look forward to its every stone and candle."

When he saw that she was asleep, when she no longer spoke to him, Gabor settled down as best he could and sighed deeply. To no one in particular, he said, "I am quite, quite tired."

The woman across the aisle from them heard a strange and disturbing snarl, but when she looked over at the two, the wolf had closed his eyes and was, to all appearances, asleep.

It was a vision of peace.

And the plane moved over the world so effortlessly it seemed unreal, as if it were a plane in a dream about planes.

28

Countess Ingrid at Home

The young woman who returned was not the girl who'd gone.

It wasn't only that Ingrid now knew more than she had, it was that she was now responsible for a (somewhat) wild and (sometimes) frightening wolf. She had to think of others, before she thought of herself.

First, Gabor needed to get out. If he did not walk or run at least twice a day, he became irritable and snapped at whomever was about. This snapping and lunging was terrifying to Krysztina, who, when Gabor was in a mood, would not stay in her own home.

It didn't matter what Ingrid said or how she felt. If he had not walked about, Gabor was likely to snap at any stranger in his path. So, every day, with Sandor's blessing, Gabor and Ingrid went for long walks: once in the morning, once in the evening.

Gabor would not hear of wearing a leash and, as no one wished to offend him, no one insisted. Besides, as he and Ingrid understood each other perfectly, a leash would have been redundant. The only problem they had was not when dogs barked at the wolf (this Gabor did not take personally), but, rather, when dogs (or people) looked as if they might interfere with Ingrid.

Gabor was inclined to attack at once. He did not understand the purpose of a "warning."

"You can't just hurt people," said Ingrid. "You have to warn them what you're going to do."

"The countess is certainly correct, but the custom makes no sense to me. If I am to break a dog's neck, it is because the dog has done something wrong. . . ."

"But maybe it doesn't know it was wrong."

"And am I to school every one who threatens the countess? The object is to prevent the dog from doing harm. Is it not more practical to kill the dog at once? Why should I warn the creature?"

"Because it's wrong to break a dog's neck."

In the end, Gabor swore not to attack anyone without Ingrid's permission, but because she could never quite convince him about warnings, Ingrid kept Gabor away from others as much as she could.

Their time together, that summer, was good for both of them. It was then that the wolf and the girl began to understand each other, then that Gabor became almost a part of Ingrid.

The only annoying side of Gabor's personality was his intense dislike of squirrels. Though he thought the poor creatures unworthy of his attention, he simply could not help himself. No sooner did a squirrel pass than he would growl and look as though he wanted to chase the creature down.

"Why don't you like squirrels?" asked Ingrid.

"This I do not know, Countess," said Gabor. "I feel they are impertinent and ugly, but so are many creatures. Perhaps squirrels are more so?"

"I don't think so," said Ingrid.

"I cannot think what else it could be," said Gabor.

As Ingrid did not want to alarm people in Parkdale, she herself cut Gabor's hair, styling it so that, from a distance, he could pass for a mutt. Once a month, she dyed his hair black.

This was all more embarrassing for her than it was for Gabor, who did not care what others thought of his appearance.

After three weeks at home, Ingrid began to learn to control her own feelings. This was a most difficult thing, but most important. If she showed the least fear of someone or the least doubt, Gabor was ready to pounce on the offender.

Once that summer, Gabor knocked down three men, all of them drunk, who lurched too close to Ingrid while they were walking along Cowan. He would have bitten them all, but one of the men, who must have been very drunk indeed, did not seem to mind that Gabor had knocked him to the pavement. He kept saying, "There's a good boy, Daddy's home," until Gabor got off him in disgust.

"I do not think he is dangerous," said Gabor.

"No," said Ingrid. "I'm sorry, Gabor. I was frightened."

"Quite rightly," said Gabor.

They walked on, but from that moment, she was careful to keep calm.

One evening, Ingrid and Gabor were walking by the side of the lake. It was near the end of August, the days growing shorter, the evening sun turning the lake pink and orange before it set. They had been talking of nothing in particular. Gabor was fascinated by the lake itself, as if he thought it might one day disappear.

He went down the stone steps and put his front paw in the water. "It is wonderful," he said.

Ingrid was not fascinated by the lake. It was such a constant presence, she took it for granted, but she hated to disappoint Gabor, so she answered, "It's pretty nice, I guess."

As she said the words, she heard: "You shouldn't let your dog put his paw in the lake, Ingrid."

And there, with her mother and her Pomeranian, was Sheila Wilson.

"Who's your friend?" asked Mrs. Wilson.

And Gabor, who knew exactly when Ingrid was upset, growled. "Shall I deal with them, Countess?"

"No," said Ingrid. "Don't hurt them."

"Allow me at least to kill the dog."

"No," said Ingrid. "You mustn't. Let *me* deal with them."

The Wilsons, mother and daughter, both of them frightened, took a step back from Ingrid and her dog. Neither said anything more. They scampered off, dragging their whimpering doglet with them.

It was a puzzling encounter, at first. Ingrid had been upset by the sight of Sheila Wilson, but she could not understand why Sheila and her mother had gone off, until she realized that the Wilsons would have heard her speaking to Gabor, would have heard her deep growls.

It must have seemed to the Wilsons that Ingrid was "not quite right."

It doesn't matter what they think, thought Ingrid.

But, after that, she was more careful in public, speaking to Gabor only when they were alone.

It had been an interesting summer. From the moment she had stepped off the plane to Budapest, Ingrid had discovered one marvel after another. How much there had been to take in: mansions, servants, a book made of salt, a labyrinth filled with crows.

Then, after three weeks in the Old Country, she had returned home with a most interesting friend: Gabor.

Ingrid had lost track of time. It was a surprise to her when her mother reminded her that, shortly, she would return to school, to grade seven.

School? thought Ingrid.

On the first day of school, Gabor would not wait for her at home. He would not let her walk to school by herself. Instead, he accompanied her and, then, waited all day, lying patiently outside the school yard, until the school day's end.

The first morning, Ingrid introduced Gabor and Alice, as if introducing her two closest friends.

That went very well. Alice was astonished at the bond between Ingrid and Gabor. "Where did you get him?" she asked.

Before Ingrid could tell her story, Sheila Wilson approached.

"I'd watch out for Ingrid," said Sheila. "My mother doesn't think she's right in the head."

Ingrid smiled at Sheila and growled.

"There, I told you," said Sheila, "and her dog's dangerous." Sheila moved away from them. "Are you coming, Alice?"

"In a minute," said Alice.

When Sheila had gone, Alice asked, "Is he really dangerous, Ingrid?"

"No," said Ingrid. "He's very nice."

"What did you do when you were on vacation?" asked Alice.

As Ingrid was about to answer, the bell rang.

"I'll tell you later," said Ingrid.

Only a year before, Ingrid might have been upset that Alice and Sheila were still friends. She might have been upset that Sheila was still at Queen Elizabeth. But the concerns of the previous year were no longer hers.

She walked Gabor to a grassy corner of the lot, on the public side of the fence.

"Are you sure you'll be okay here?"

"Quite comfortable," said Gabor.

The wolf lay down on the lawn.

"I'll see you at lunchtime," said Ingrid.

And she walked towards school, wondering if it was right to leave him where he was. Would he be more comfortable inside the school yard? What would he do in winter?

Since leaving the Old Country, she hadn't thought of money or inheritance. Since leaving the Old Country, she thought most about Gabor. How important he was to her. What was the title of her chapter in *A History of the Balazses*? "Ingrid Countess Balazs and the End of Gabor." She had thought about that title often, with great sadness. She knew, and Gabor easily accepted, that he would die, but it did not seem possible that such a strong and wonderful friend should ever go.

What seemed strange was that there had ever been a time when he was *not* part of her life. Once, as they were walking along Springhurst, she had said to him, "I hope you live forever, Gabor. I'm sorry you came from your home."

And he'd said, "The countess need not concern herself on my behalf. I am grateful. I have enjoyed our time together more than all my years in the labyrinth."

Before she stepped into the school, Ingrid looked back at the wolf.

He was looking at her, unwavering, as she went in.

Acknowledgment

Without the
intelligence and inspiration of
Catherine Bush,
this book would not have been written.
Catherine first suggested I write
a children's novel and,
then, she helped to
edit this
one.
I am deeply grateful.